A Candlelight
Regency Special

Diamonds and the Arrogant Rake

Anne Hillary

A CANDLELIGHT REGENCY SPECIAL

Published by
Dell Publishing Co., Inc.
1 Dag Hammarskjold Plaza
New York, New York 10017

Copyright © 1982 by Anne Kolaczyk

All rights reserved. No part of this book may be
reproduced or transmitted in any form or by any
means, electronic or mechanical, including photocopying,
recording or by any information storage
and retrieval system, without the written permission
of the Publisher, except where permitted by law.

Dell ® TM 681510, Dell Publishing Co., Inc.

ISBN: 0-440-12094-2

Printed in the United States of America
First printing—March 1982

Diamonds and the Arrogant Rake

CHAPTER ONE

"For God's sake, do you think I enjoy feeling like a fool?" His Grace the duke of Herriad shouted at the young man lounging in the chair before him. "I did not know what to say to that woman or her sniveling daughter. They were ready to send a notice of your engagement to Isabella to the *Gazette*."

Lord Waring, the duke's only son and heir, looked impatient with the proceedings. His exquisitely clad body was sprawled across a nearby chair, the picture of relaxation, but his dark brown eyes flashed with irritation. "Somehow, though, I feel sure that you dissuaded them."

"It was not easy," the duke said, shaking his head. He was as tall as his son, with the same muscular build, but the similarities ended there. Besides the fact that the duke's dark hair was now streaked with gray, there was a basic difference between the two men. Where His Grace was always composed in a cold, formal way, his son's manner was more easy and flippant, though most people were charmed by it rather than offended. "Mrs. Hartnett was in a towering rage. Whatever possessed you to become involved with an innocent young girl?" he asked, more in exasperation than expectation of an answer.

His son laughed loudly and stood up. "Isabella Hartnett is about as innocent as I am. I think she spent the whole evening out in the garden with various men."

"How was it, then, that you were the only one found with her?" his father snapped.

Lord Waring shrugged his shoulders with a smile that would have set any female heart aflutter, but which only irritated his father even more. "How do we know I was the only one? Perhaps I was deemed most eligible."

The duke silently conceded that possibility but continued to glare unforgivingly at his son. "That does not change the fact that you put me in an intolerable position, and I do not intend to let you do that again."

"What do you expect me to do? Beg your forgiveness and promise to reform my sinful life?" the young man asked cynically as he walked across the room to a window. He pulled aside the heavy red velvet curtain and looked down into the garden below.

"I merely expect the excuse I gave Mrs. Hartnett to become the truth," the duke said.

The drapery fell back in place as Lord Waring

turned to his father. "And what is that?" he asked with barely concealed boredom.

His father rose to his feet, leaning his hands on the desk before him. "I told her that you could not marry Isabella because you were already pledged to another."

"And she believed that?" Lord Waring laughed incredulously.

"Yes, she did. And by September it will be true."

The young man's humor disappeared. "We have been through this all before," he said with annoyance. "I do not intend to marry just because you think it is time." He turned and strode angrily toward the door.

"Alex," his father called him back.

Alex turned at the doorway, his hand on the knob.

"I am not giving you a choice. I want you married by September."

"And how do you intend to force me?" Alex asked coldly.

His father sat down slowly, his eyes never leaving his son's. "I shall change my will."

A look of relief passed across Alex's face. "Have you forgotten about the entailment?" he asked smoothly.

"No," his father said, shaking his head. "I am well aware that you'll get the two country estates regardless of any will I make, but I am also aware that their income would barely keep you in boot polish for a year."

Alex took his hand off the knob. "Just what are you saying?"

"I'm saying that if you don't marry by September, I shall leave everything I own that is not entailed to someone else, and that includes this house and all my money."

"That's pitching it too rum," Alex scoffed, his face slightly pale. "You would never leave this house to someone outside the family. You waited too long to buy it back after grandfather sold it to pay off his debts. You would never let it go."

His Grace picked up a small penknife and idly turned it about in his hand. "I never said I would leave it to someone outside the family," he pointed out quietly.

"Then what the—" Alex stopped suddenly. "You don't mean you'd leave it to Elizabeth?"

"Yes. I'd rather leave it to that vulgar, scheming hussy of a cousin of yours than continue to watch our name be dragged through the mud by you." He put the penknife down suddenly and stood up. "I mean it, Alex. Three months."

Alex glared at him angrily and reached for the doorknob. "Three months or three years, your threats matter nothing to me! The devil take you and your money!" he cried and threw himself from the room.

His Grace sat down heavily, listening to his son's exit from the house. He had known that Alex would not take the ultimatum well, but he was quite serious about it. To the duke, marriage seemed the only way left to save his son from the life of ruin that he appeared bent on leading.

Ever since Alex had returned from the army, he had thrown himself into the most disreputable parts of the London social life. He gambled heavily in the most notorious gaming dens and made no secret of his liaisons with various married women in society. At first his father had said nothing, assuming that it was a kind of release for him after the horrors of the war in France. But it was three years now, and Alex was showing no signs of changing. His Grace was no longer able to hide his disapproval, and the rift between them seemed to be growing wider each day.

His father was not one to shrug off his son's behavior, though, and he continually sought a way to bring Alex to his senses. This time he was sure that he had succeeded. Alex was a man of twenty-five. If he settled down with a wife and family, he would forget his wild ways. If only he would find some nice quiet young lady and leave the scandals to someone else.

Alex was livid with rage as he walked from his father's house. He did not intend to obey him, but he had the uneasy feeling that his father was quite determined this time.

Blast that Isabella Hartnett, he thought silently as he dodged a carriage and crossed the street. She certainly had not been worth all the trouble she had caused. And just for a few kisses, too! You'd think, from the way they all acted, that he had ravished her! She was not as innocent as her mother hoped she was, if her expertise at kissing was any indication.

Alex nodded silently to an acquaintance who passed him, wondering what had suddenly driven his father to such madness. This was not the first time he had tried to force his son into marriage, but he had never resorted to threats before.

Actually, Alex thought with a cynical smile, just a few years ago he had been quite ready to marry. When he had returned home from the peninsula, all he had wanted was to wed a neighbor girl whom he had dreamed about the whole time he was in the army. It had been quite a blow to discover that she had married one of his friends in the meantime, but even worse to realize that she was willing to have an affair with him. Stunned that the perfect angel of his dreams would act in such a way, he had refused her offer quite coldly.

Once he was back in London, though, he had discovered that she was no different from most of the women in society. Married to one man, they would seek the attentions of any who took their fancy. Alex was young, handsome and wealthy, and he soon found himself the center of much female attention. He was not so naive as to believe they cared about him, but neither was he so foolish as to scorn their invitations.

Now, having spent three years sampling their pleasures, he was no longer the foolish young man who had returned from the army. He did not dream of finding a sweet young girl in whose loyalty and love he could find happiness, for he knew such a creature did not exist.

Even though he had barely been aware of his surroundings, Alex's feet had taken him to a quiet-looking house on Half Moon Street. He knocked sharply on the door, his foot tapping impatiently as he waited for it to be opened.

An expressionless butler opened the door and stepped aside for him to enter. "My lady is expecting you, my lord," he said as he took Alex's hat and cane. "She is in her room."

Nodding slightly, Alex went up the stairs. How the devil did Morgana know he was coming? He hadn't expected to see her at all today. She must be quite sure of her charms.

A maid just coming out of Morgana's bedroom held the door open for him, curtsying shyly. He pushed past her and stopped short as he entered the room. Several other maids were bustling about, and a dressmaker was busily making alterations on a dress Morgana was wearing. Blast, he silently cursed. Just what he needed—a domestic scene.

"Alex, darling," Morgana purred when she caught sight of him in the doorway. "How wonderful to see you." She floated across the room and took his hand. "I had so hoped you would come by today."

Glancing quickly at the others in the room, Alex smiled slightly. He disliked conducting his affairs as publicly as Morgana seemed to want to. However, that was an easy fault to overlook when one considered all her assets. He watched her as she chased the others from the room.

Lady Morgana Tremayne was a tall woman who possessed considerable beauty and charm and absolutely no morals. She had flaming red hair that fell halfway down her back. Her large, green eyes were fringed with heavy, dark lashes. Moving with sensuous grace, she knew the power of her full breasts and long legs.

Lord Francis Tremayne, her third husband, had been chosen, like the others, for his wealth and ill health. It was rumored that he was near death at his country estate, but that did not stop Morgana from pursuing her pleasures in town.

Once the door had closed and they were alone, Morgana pulled Alex to the edge of the bed. "London has become unbelievably dreary," she sighed. "The end of the season is so utterly depressing that I always wonder why I didn't leave a week or two earlier. But then I would miss the last parties." Her voice died away in indecision.

"Life certainly can be difficult," Alex remarked. Looking about him, he noticed her trunks open, as if she was in the midst of packing. "Are you going to Berkshire to see Francis?"

Morgana laughed in real amusement. "Whatever for? Surely you don't expect me to hold his hand and wipe his brow!"

"Heaven forbid!" Alex murmured. "Think of the parties you might miss!"

She chose to ignore his sarcasm. "Now if you were ill and needed me, that would be different," she purred, sliding her hand across his chest and tugging at his cravat. "I would stay by your side and nurse you constantly."

Alex stood up abruptly and walked a few feet to her dressing table, where he idly looked at the jewelry scattered carelessly about. "I think nursing Francis would be far more profitable. He's much more likely to reward your devotion than I am."

Her eyes narrowed in irritation at his impatient tone, but her voice was soft and only gently scolding. "I vow!" she said and laughed sadly. "You are most provoking today. I hope you don't intend to be so ill tempered in Brighton or I shall cry off." A look of worry passed quickly over her face. "There isn't any problem about the house I wanted, is there?"

"No, no. I told you I had rented the one you admired so last summer." Her self-centeredness only irritated him further, and he spoke more roughly than he had intended.

Her full lips pursed slightly as she looked at him worriedly. "Then what have I done to offend you?"

Alex sighed. He knew her injured air was just an act, but still, it was not fair to take out his anger on her. He came back to her side and picked up her hand. "I'm sorry. I've been a brute and I know it." He kissed it lightly, then stood up and walked restlessly about her room. "I've had a royal set-to with my father, but that's no reason to behave shabbily toward you."

Morgana's eyes widened in interest. Despising the duke, she was delighted that there were problems between him and Alex, and she would happily do anything to aggravate them.

She had first met the duke of Herriad almost seven years ago, when Morgana had been Mrs. Elsworth, a grieving widowed bride. Her poor darling Clarence, only a spritely sixty-four, had succumbed to heart failure on their honeymoon in Ireland. She bore her sudden loss bravely, admitting to all that she would trade the whole Elsworth fortune just to have her dear Clarence back again. Her halo began to tarnish slightly, though, as Clarence's relatives seemed to pop out from every corner, all trying to grab a share of his money. To make matters worse, it was discovered that the fool had not changed his will to include her! By the time she had hired a lawyer to protect her interests, she realized that she would have to search for another husband.

Although she preferred wealthy old men, when she met the duke of Herriad, she began to wonder if there might not be some value in a live husband. The duke was handsome, but more than that attracted her to him. Perhaps it was the way other women tried so hard to catch his interest but always failed. Or it might have been that she envied the attention and respect he received from other members of society and wanted some of it for herself. Whatever her reason, Morgana decided that she would succeed where others had failed.

Since she had been using her body to attract men from the age of fifteen, Morgana never doubted that the duke would eventually succumb to her charms. But the more she tried, the more disdainful he became. Although he was cool to her in public, Morgana took heart from the fact that he never actually snubbed her. With some subtle maneuvering she managed to get him alone at a ball. Rather than being grateful for the chance to open his heart to her, he had called her a bold, vulgar piece and suggested that she had windmills in her head if she thought he would ever consider any sort of alliance with her. Morgana did the only thing possible for someone in her position. She quickly married Mr. Claude Amesbury, who, although he was not quite ready to slip the wind, was fifty-eight and looking poorly.

Unluckily, the idea of such a comely bride had caused Claude to recover miraculously, and he lived for four blissful years before tragically choking on a fish bone. Once more Morgana had bravely donned her widow's weeds, secure in the knowledge that Claude had no relatives and that he had changed his will after they were married. Unfortunately, he had added a clause that gave her only a small allowance unless she remained unwed for ten years after his death.

After only the briefest of mourning periods, Morgana had returned to town. The fine clothes and rich life she desired had eluded her once more, but she was ready to try again. The duke of Herriad was still active in society, but she turned up her pretty little nose at him and looked about for her next husband.

Lord Francis Tremayne had already outlived four wives of his own and had six daughters but no sons. His doctor insisted that if he wanted a son, he must marry a very young woman. Unfortunately, all the very young women he found had fathers who objected to a sixty-eight-year-old man courting their daughters. Morgana was the youngest woman who took him seriously. After promising her a substantial part of his fortune on their wedding day, he was able to convince her to marry him.

Lord Francis's much desired son never materialized, and Morgana at last had the wealth and the freedom she desired. She should have been quite content, but a lingering shadow remained—she had never forgiven the duke of Herriad for his rejection of her, and she vowed revenge.

Alex's disillusionment gave her the perfect chance. Although he was handsome and charming enough to make her want him for his own sake, he was also Herriad's only son and heir. Experience had made him bitter and cynical, and she would encourage those feelings until Francis finally died. By then she should have enough control over Alex to make him her next husband. Herriad would be sorry then.

Alex, meanwhile, had no idea that she had such

far-reaching plans. He thought she was an enjoyable companion, even if a bit more demanding than some of the others he had dallied with. Although he found her careless attitude about Francis's impending death distasteful, he foresaw no threat to himself when she was eventually widowed again.

As Alex wandered about her room, Morgana watched uneasily, wondering just what their quarrel had been about. She never doubted that it somehow involved her. "Did your father find out about Brighton?" she asked with concern.

Alex looked at her in surprise. "Brighton?" What was there to find out about Brighton? Their relationship there would be the same as it had been in London. All he had done was make the arrangements for her to rent a house she admired. "No, no," he said, shaking his head. "He's got some fool notion that I must marry. Before September, or he'll leave his money to someone else."

Morgana jumped to her feet, trying to control her agitation. "He's not serious?"

Alex nodded grimly. "Oh, that he is. He's named my cousin Elizabeth as his new heir if I fail."

Sitting down slowly, Morgana's forehead was creased with a frown. "Elizabeth? I didn't know you had any relatives."

"Oh, yes," he said, turning to gaze absently out the window. "I have never met her, but Father could barely express his dislike of her the one time he saw her."

"It seems odd that he would leave his fortune to someone he hates," Morgana said slowly. Watching Alex carefully, she tried to judge his reaction to his father's ultimatum. "What is this cousin like? A crotchety old maid?"

Alex shrugged. "Apparently."

Morgana knew how close September was and wondered frantically if Francis would have died by that time. Even if he died tomorrow, there would hardly be sufficient time for a mourning period. Although she thought such customs were ridiculous, one had to follow them if one wanted to be accepted in the right circles. Blast that Herriad! He was managing to thwart her again!

"It would serve him right if you married this crusty old cousin he hates!" Morgana complained bitterly.

"What?" Alex spun around to stare at her.

"Oh, I was only joking," she said with a shrug. "But I would love to see his little scheme backfire."

Alex turned slowly back to the window. "Yes," he murmured thoughtfully, "so would I."

Morgana came up behind him and slid her arms around his waist. "Let's forget about him, shall we? I'm sure that you didn't come here just to tell me you had argued with your father."

Turning around in her arms, Alex smiled down at her. "That would be quite a waste of your charms, now wouldn't it?" He bent his head to meet her waiting lips, having apparently forgotten all about his father's threats.

By that evening Alex's rage had faded to a quiet anger. He and a friend, Sir Matthew Denby, went to a long-awaited prizefight at the Fives Court in St. Martin's Street, but Alex found it difficult to appreciate the bout. Even the wine he and Denby liberally consumed did not help. Morgana's joking suggestion kept creeping back into his mind until he was forced to admit that it might be the perfect answer to his problem.

"Have you ever heard of a town named Welford?" Alex suddenly turned to Denby to ask as they walked down St. Martin's Street after the fight. It was starting to rain lightly, and he tried to wave down a hackney. It passed them by.

"Welford?" Denby asked in surprise, for his mind, if not Alex's, had been on the fight they had just seen. "Is there to be a turn-up there?"

"No, no," Alex said quickly. He tried in vain to hail another passing hackney. "My father's cousin lives there, and I was considering a visit."

Denby shook his head with a frown. The movement almost knocked him over, since the wine had left him unsteady. He reached out a hand to steady himself. "You had better watch out when you're visiting families. They always want you to marry some friend of theirs they've got tucked away."

"Is that so bad?" Alex asked lightly.

"Have you lost your senses?" Denby was shocked. "They'll be putting you in Bedlam soon if you aren't careful!"

Alex just laughed, putting his arm around the other man's shoulders. "But think about it, Denby," he said. "Aren't you planning on wedding some day?"

He shrugged.

"I imagine that most of us will," Alex answered for him. "The real trick is to find the perfect woman."

"And you have?" Denby asked suspiciously.

"No, not I," Alex denied quickly. Another hackney came down the street, and he waved it to a stop. The two men got in before Alex spoke again. "Suppose you found a woman who hated London society, who had never been near town because she preferred life in the country."

"She wouldn't pester the life out of you to take her about," Denby pointed out.

"Exactly. Nor would she interfere with any other plans you had already made," Alex said meaningfully. "Plus she could be brought to town when you needed protection from all those matchmaking mothers who want you to marry their little innocents."

"But she probably wouldn't discourage the little innocents," Denby laughed.

"And suppose there was a strong possibility that

she would inherit a fortune in the future," Alex continued.

"That would help ease the bondage considerably."

"But best of all," Alex leaned forward and whispered gleefully, "suppose she was the one person that your domineering father would hate to see you marry?"

"I'd marry her in a second," Denby shouted happily.

Alex leaned back in the carriage. "And that's exactly what I shall do," he said quietly.

CHAPTER TWO

"The poor woman was so ill during the winter, and she isn't really much better now. When I saw the delicious pigeon pie that Bertha had made for our dinner, I knew that was just what Mrs. Lane needed."

Elizabeth looked up from the household accounts she was struggling over and turned to face her mother, a worried frown creasing her forehead. "So . . ." she prompted.

Margaret Corbett put down her embroidery and smiled at her daughter. "So I sent it over to her."

Trying hard to suppress a groan, Elizabeth smiled weakly at her mother. "I'm sure Mrs. Lane will appreciate it."

Mrs. Corbett's eyes narrowed slightly as she looked at her daughter more closely, suspecting her of sarcasm. "It's not as if we really needed that pie," she scolded lightly. "We have more than enough for ourselves, and we ought to share with those around us."

"Yes, of course, Mother." Elizabeth nodded wearily. She turned back to the papers before her with little enthusiasm. She could hardly begrudge some nourishing food to an old sick woman. Besides, she thought dejectedly, it was not as if that one pie were going to make any difference in the columns of figures in front of her. She rubbed her forehead absently, leaving a smudge of ink where her fingers had been.

Margaret returned to her sewing. "I know that my gifts irritate you sometimes," she continued rather apologetically. "But we aren't exactly destitute."

Elizabeth glanced around the room, her eyes taking in the worn upholstery on the chairs, the threadbare spots in the carpeting and the places where the sun had rotted holes in the drapery. How was it her mother never noticed what appalling conditions they lived in?

"And with the money we get from your father's investments," Margaret continued, "we have more than we need." She finished the tiny pink rosebud she was embroidering and put the material down in her lap. "You know, I was so surprised to learn that he had made those investments. It didn't seem like him at all."

Elizabeth turned away quickly, hoping that her mother had not noticed her suddenly flushed cheeks. "Perhaps he did it while he was foxed," she said lightly.

"Elizabeth!" Her mother was shocked. "That's no

way to speak of your father! Whatever his faults, he provided very well for us after his death."

Better than he ever did while he was alive, Elizabeth thought grimly. She suddenly grew tired of trying to find extra guineas hidden somewhere between the rows of her neat figures. Crumpling up the papers, she threw them across the table.

"Oh, I didn't mean to anger you," Margaret cried remorsefully, and she hurried across the room to her daughter's side, putting her hand pleadingly on Elizabeth's arm. "I shouldn't have said what I did. I didn't mean to sound scolding."

"I'm not angry with you." Elizabeth laughed and, standing up, gently hugged her mother. She was quite a bit taller than Margaret and sometimes felt more like her older sister than her daughter. Over Margaret's head, she caught sight of the dress she was trimming with little flowers, lying on the floor forgotten. "Oh, now look what you've done!" she teased. Her mother turned in the direction that Elizabeth was looking. "I know we have more money than we can ever possibly spend, but you needn't throw my new dress on the floor."

"Oh, my goodness!" Margaret cried and hurried over to rescue the dress. She shook out the soft white muslin and folded it carefully over her arm. "I should be finished with it soon," she promised. "And then we must invite Mr. Crewe over for tea. I cannot wait to see his face when he sees you in this. I'll wager he'll be begging for your hand before the evening is over."

Elizabeth smiled at her mother, although Mr. Crewe's excitement over her new dress was hard to imagine. She personally doubted his ability to become excited over anything, but she kept that to herself and helped her mother gather together her embroidery silks.

Elizabeth suspected that her mother would think highly of any man who showed even the faintest interest in courting her. She smiled suddenly, picturing Margaret serving tea and making idle conversation with a highwayman still wearing his mask and carrying a smoking gun.

Of course, Mr. Crewe was totally respectable. He was their vicar, widowed with four young children. His wife had been dead for almost a year and a half now, and lately he had gotten into the habit of stopping by for tea on Thursday afternoons.

Margaret found him quite eligible and openly approved of his visits, for she felt it was time her daughter had a home and family of her own. Since her husband's death, Margaret had been drifting along in a pleasant sort of daze. Elizabeth had been fifteen at the time, but she had admirably stepped in and taken over. Margaret had readily admitted to herself that it was a great relief not to be the one hounded by their creditors, for she had never known what to say to them and had flustered about nervously. Elizabeth never had that problem. She dealt with everyone coolly and calmly. Of course, once she had found the papers telling them about Timothy's investments, things became much easier. Margaret did not have to be afraid to go into town if she wanted to. The merchants were all helpful, polite and quite willing to settle her accounts with Elizabeth later, as if there hadn't been a time when they had refused to deal with her unless she had the cash right with her to pay for what she wanted.

Then, suddenly, one cold day in the past winter, Margaret had looked at her daughter and realized that Elizabeth was not a middle-aged woman like herself. She was young—only twenty—yet she dressed in plain, drab dresses that only emphasized her height and slender figure. Her lovely chestnut brown hair was scraped back as if she were an old maid. Margaret was immediately consumed with guilt. Her dependence was causing her daughter to miss all the fun a young girl was supposed to have. She decided to do something about it.

At first Elizabeth had been reluctant to change. Her clothes were fine, she had protested, and so was her hair. Margaret had been stubborn, though, and Elizabeth had finally allowed her to sew several more flattering dresses for her. She would have them made, however, only as she needed new dresses, for there was no reason to toss away perfectly good dresses just because they were not fashionable. She did agree to try a new hairstyle that her mother suggested, but she did not see that it made much difference in how she looked.

Although Margaret and their housekeeper Bertha had loudly fussed over Elizabeth, the town of Welford had not noticed the suddenly fashionable Miss Corbett. Elizabeth had thought it funny and had not been able to resist teasing her mother, who had expected lines of suitors to begin forming at the door.

After a bit, though, it became apparent that someone had noticed. Each Sunday after services, Mr. Crewe made a point of speaking to them. Margaret was quick to invite him to tea, and he was equally quick to accept.

Although nothing was ever said, Elizabeth assumed that one day she would marry him. It was not a very exciting prospect, but she was not exactly overwhelmed with suitors from whom to choose, and she could not expect her mother to support her forever. She knew exactly what life as a vicar's wife would be like and what would be expected of her. She would perform her duties adequately and, in return, she would receive security and respect—things her mother had never received from her father.

As her mother packed her silks into her sewing basket, Elizabeth caught sight of the crumpled accounts lying on the table across the room. With a sigh she realized what she was going to have to do, and she turned back to her mother. "Were you going up to your room to rest before dinner?" she asked.

"I thought I would, unless you don't want me to."

Margaret looked up at her daughter, a puzzled expression on her face.

"Oh, no," Elizabeth said quickly, slipping her arm over her mother's shoulders. "I know you didn't sleep well last night, and the rest will do you good. I was just going to suggest using my room instead of yours."

Her mother looked even more puzzled.

"Your room is so hot this time of day," Elizabeth continued, "while mine usually has a breeze to cool it off."

"I didn't realize that," Margaret said as they walked out of the parlor into a small hallway. "That's odd, since they are next to one another."

"Yes, isn't it?" Elizabeth laughed nervously.

They had reached the bottom of the stairway, and Margaret went up a step. She turned and patted her daughter's hand. "You are always so thoughtful of me," she smiled. "You will make a wonderful wife and mother one of these days."

Elizabeth smiled back but did not feel like the saint her mother seemed to think she was. She stood at the bottom of the stairway watching until she saw the door to her bedroom close. She went back to the parlor and picked up the papers she had scattered about, listening all the while for sounds from upstairs.

Almost half an hour passed, and the house was quite still except for occasional noises from the kitchen, where Bertha was working. Elizabeth knew she ought to see if Bertha had enough ingredients to scrape together a meal, but there were more pressing matters to attend to first.

Walking silently up the stairs, Elizabeth eased open the door of her room just a few inches. The drapes had been pulled, but in the dim light she could see her mother lying on the bed. From the sounds of her even breathing, Elizabeth decided she must be asleep.

Elizabeth closed the door as quietly as possible and hurried to the next door. She opened it quickly and rushed inside. It was silly, she knew, but she still felt guilty sneaking about as she had to. She was only doing it because they needed the money so badly, but she was aware that her mother would never approve of her actions.

Going to the wardrobe on the far side of the room, Elizabeth carefully lifted out the boxes and bags stored on the top shelf. That was an advantage of being taller that her mother, she thought with a sudden grin. A safe-out-of-sight hiding place to her mother was still right before her eyes.

At the back of the shelf lay a small wooden box, covered with dust. Elizabeth glanced nervously about, then pulled it forward. She fumbled slightly with the catch but managed to open it on the second try. Then, pushing back the top, she exposed a small bundle wrapped in old, yellowed velvet. Without further hesitation Elizabeth pulled the piece of velvet apart and lifted out a necklace.

The sunlight coming in through her mother's window caught the diamonds in the necklace, and rainbows of color suddenly danced about the room. Elizabeth could not resist holding it up for a moment, marveling at how the quiet little stones seemed to hold a fire inside them. But she had not taken them out to admire them and only allowed herself that pleasure for a few brief seconds. Then she slipped the necklace into a pocket in her dress and closed the box, carefully arranging the velvet inside as it had been. She replaced the box on the shelf and put her mother's things back in front of it. Then she sped out of the room and down the stairs.

Elizabeth could feel the weight of the necklace against her hip as she walked and knew that her face was flushed from nervousness. Forcing herself to slow her pace slightly, she went into the kitchen.

Bertha looked up from the long wooden table where she was slicing vegetables. "Yer mother gave away yer dinner," she said grimly.

Elizabeth nodded. "Yes, she told me." She looked about the room to see what was being prepared. "Have you enough food for dinner?"

Bertha glanced up at her with a scowl. "Aye, but jest barely."

Ignoring her forbidding look, Elizabeth reached over and hugged the old lady. "Darling Bertha, I knew you would manage. You always do when Mother does something like this."

"Ya ought ta tell her ta stop givin' everythin'

away," Bertha grumbled. The only sign that she had even noticed Elizabeth's hug was the bright red spot in the middle of each cheek. She continued to slice the potatoes into a large pot.

Elizabeth picked up a slice of carrot that had missed the pot and munched on it thoughtfully. "Where's Ben? Do you know?"

Bertha's shrewd dark eyes flew up to Elizabeth, who tried to meet her look with one of total innocence, but she could not control the guilty flush that crept into her cheeks.

" 'Spect he's in ta garden," Bertha muttered as she returned to her work.

Elizabeth nodded and sauntered casually toward the door. She could not help taking a glance back at Bertha, but the cook was busy working and appeared to have forgotten that Elizabeth was still there. She was being silly, Elizabeth scolded herself. How could Bertha know what she was doing?

Letting herself out the back door, Elizabeth looked about their yard. It was not very large, for they just had a small piece of property on the edge of town, but Ben had transformed the grounds behind the house into a wonderful garden. Wide beds of flowers grew around a small terrace where she and her mother liked to sit in the evenings. Behind the flowers were rows and rows of vegetables; more than enough for their needs for the whole year. She spotted Ben working in a far corner.

She walked a few feet down the small stone path

that wandered through the garden, and then she stopped. Ben looked up and rose to his feet when he saw her there. She turned suddenly and went into the old building that used to be the stables when they had been able to afford horses. Now Ben used it for storage and had made a small corner of it into a workroom. It was to this small corner that she went.

A wide table filled the corner, and dusty shelves rose behind it. Elizabeth reached purposefully for a large, cracked flowerpot on a top shelf and pulled a small bag out from inside it. She loosened the string that held it closed and spilled delicate-looking metal tools onto the table top.

A shadow in the doorway blocked out the sun for a moment, then Elizabeth heard Ben's uneven steps as he crossed the room to her side.

"Why don't ya jest tell her she can't be givin' yer food away?" he said with a sigh.

Elizabeth had taken the necklace from her pocket and laid it across the table. She straightened it out so that the stones were lying faceup. Even in the musty, dim old shed they sparkled and shone with a life of their own. She picked up a small knife and carefully began to pry up the tiny metal prongs that held one stone in place.

"One dinner didn't do it, Ben," she said slowly, concentrating on her work. "I've known it was coming for weeks now." She succeeded in moving one prong away from the stone. "And we've really done quite well. It's been almost six months since we sold that last stone, and we all got new clothes out of the money."

Ben watched in silence for a few moments, and Elizabeth could sense his disapproval. "Ya still should tell her," he insisted.

"No," Elizabeth said firmly, glancing up at him as she spoke. "She had enough worries when he was alive. She doesn't need them now. I'll take care of things." Another prong was raised.

"Ya gonna want me ta go tanight?" Ben said as he moved slowly over to an old chair in the corner.

"No, wait until the morning," she said, smiling at him with real affection. Ben had been with them for ten years now. He and Bertha were like family to her.

"Do ya really feel this is wise, lass?" Ben asked her quietly as she freed the stone at last from the confines of the setting. She lifted it carefully away from the necklace, then turned to look at him.

"How else would we get money for food?" she challenged him. "My father left us nothing but debts, debts and more debts." The bitterness in her voice was clear.

"But ta take the jools like this." Ben shook his gray head. "It's gonta catch up with ya one of these days."

"Oh, Ben." Elizabeth laughed lightly but was unable to completely hide her tension from Ben. "How will I get caught? Mother never wears this necklace. I think she has forgotten about it."

"What about when the stones are gone?" he asked.

She shrugged her shoulders. "We've sold five in the last five years, and two of them were to pay off Father's debts. With the stones that are left, we can live comfortably for twenty or thirty more years. Mother can be happy for the rest of her life."

"But ya should tell her where the money's from," he persisted.

"No!" Elizabeth cried, grimly determined. "You saw how he humiliated her with his gambling and other women." She saw Ben's lips tighten. "Yes, I knew about them. Everyone knew about them. And I knew how sick Mother was that one winter when we had no money for a warm cloak for her. We only had money to pay the doctor because I took it from Father's coat when he passed out, dead drunk in the parlor. She's suffered enough. It's time she had some peace. Besides," she added gently, knowing Ben was worried, "after she dies, the necklace will be mine anyway. What's the harm in using some of my inheritance now?"

Ben straightened up and shook his head. "There'll be nothing left for ya by that time."

"I shall be a staid, respectable housewife by that time and won't need them." She shrugged, unconcerned. Elizabeth carefully removed a small square of muslin from the bag of tools and wrapped the stone in it. Then she put it into the bag and dropped the loose tools into the flowerpot. When she turned, Ben was staring out the doorway. She walked slowly to his side.

"You don't have to take the stone to sell if you really feel this is wrong," she said quietly.

Ben turned to her, a look of wry humor in his eyes. He took the bag from her and slipped the long cord over his head, tucking the bag safely inside his shirt. "And how would ya know if ya was gettin' the best price?" he said. "And where ta go fer a paste stone fer the necklace? No, lass, I don't like it, but I'll do it fer ya."

"Thank you, Ben." She smiled happily and leaned over to kiss his stubby cheek. "I don't know how we'd manage without you."

Ben was immune to her flattery. He irritably wiped his cheek and glared at her. "Ya'd find some other fool, I 'spect." He turned and walked slowly back to where he had been working.

CHAPTER THREE

Welford was even smaller and duller than Alex had imagined, he thought a week later as he booked a room in the only inn in town, a tiny place called the Golden Boar.

"Will yer be staying long, me lord?" the fat little innkeeper asked, eyeing Alex with lively curiosity.

Normally loath to confide in such common folk, Alex forced himself to smile. Charming the local bumpkins often helped convince spinsters of one's sincerity. "I'm here to visit some relatives of mine," he confided. "Perhaps you know them—the Corbetts."

The innkeeper was excited. "Why, that I do. That I do!"

How could you not when this fool town must have only ten people living here, Alex thought, but his smile was carefully interested.

After changing into a splendid outfit of nankeen breeches and a deep brown coat, he asked the innkeeper for directions and was on his way.

The house was easy to find, and an elderly housekeeper who was quite impressed by his appearance let him in. Announcing his arrival with barely suppressed excitement, she was given a gracious smile as he was shown into the room.

A small woman who looked to be in her late thirties stood up hesitantly as Alex was announced. She was dressed in a pale blue dress that was attractive, though horribly out of fashion. Watching him almost fearfully, she did not seem overjoyed to meet him.

"You must be my cousin Margaret," he said with a purposefully warm smile. She nodded slightly as he took her hand and kissed it. "I am honored that you consented to see me."

Margaret pulled her hand away nervously. "It is kind of you to call on us, my lord," she murmured politely.

Turning next to the younger woman in the room, Alex smiled determinedly, ignoring the fact that she was too tall and thin to be even passably attractive and that her scraped-back hair and ugly brown dress made her look more like a kitchen maid than a woman any man with eyes in his head would choose to court. He fought down a shudder of horror as he reached for her hand.

"And I know you must be my cousin Elizabeth," he said, kissing her hand lightly but with every evidence of delight. "I have heard so much about you."

She did not become flustered and blushing as she

should have but continued to stare at him, totally unimpressed.

A round little man suddenly came forward from the corner chair where he had been sitting.

"Lord Waring," Margaret said in a strained voice, "this is our vicar, Mr. Crewe."

Mr. Crewe's head bobbed up and down with pleasure as he greeted the new arrival. Although Alex was careful to greet the man politely, he was annoyed that only the vicar seemed genuinely glad to meet him.

"What brings you to Welford?" Elizabeth asked suspiciously.

Smiling his most heart-melting smile at her, he shrugged his shoulders. "I was just traveling through town when I remembered that you lived here. I decided to be presumptuous and call on you." He turned to smile at Margaret.

Margaret twisted her hands together nervously under his regard and glanced at her daughter.

Before Elizabeth could speak again, Mr. Crewe leaned forward eagerly. "Elizabeth never told me that she had any relatives," he said. "I had no idea her family was so highly placed."

Alex darted a quick look at Elizabeth. So it was she that Mr. Crewe was here to court; not that she looked very pleased with him now. Alex turned back to the vicar, prepared to take advantage of Elizabeth's anger to rid himself of this unwanted competitor.

"Surely, as a man of the cloth, you must judge people by their inner qualities, not by the titles in their family." Alex's mouth was curved into a faint smile, but his eyes were cold.

Mr. Crewe looked taken aback. "That was not what I meant," he flustered. His face became red, and his mouth opened and closed soundlessly.

Elizabeth looked annoyed at his ineffectiveness. "No one here ever doubted your integrity," she snapped impatiently.

Mr. Crewe leaned back in his chair, looking quite injured, but Elizabeth barely noticed, for she had turned back to Alex.

"Welford seems a long way from London for you to be just passing through," she noted.

"Well, I didn't leave town this morning on a leisurely ride through the countryside and find myself in the area, if that's what you mean." He laughed good-naturedly. Lord, she was going to be a trial.

The elderly housekeeper knocked on the door and brought in an extra cup. Margaret thanked her politely and, ever the proper hostess despite the unexpected situation, poured Alex's tea and offered him some cake.

"You are staying in the area, then?" Mr. Crewe asked coldly.

Alex nodded, noting the way Margaret's eyes flew up fearfully to meet his. He put down his teacup. "For the night, at least," he said. "I have a room at the Golden Boar."

"You should be quite comfortable there," Mr. Crewe agreed, slightly more affable. "Although their cook will be busy helping prepare food for His Grace's garden party."

Alex looked a trifle confused, but Elizabeth shook her head at the vicar. "That would hardly inconvenience him if he's only staying the night. The party is still several days away."

"It sounds as if I have arrived just in time for a large social event," Alex said to Margaret, successfully feigning interest in their dull little party.

Margaret hoped that someone else might rush to answer, but his lordship was obviously waiting for her to speak. "Every year His Grace gives a garden party for his friends in the area," she said.

"Hardly his friends, Mother," Elizabeth scoffed as she poured more tea for the vicar. "He simply tries to repay all his local obligations at one time."

"But he is quite generous in hiring help for the affair," Mr. Crewe hurried to remind her. "Most of the town benefits in some way from it."

Alex watched as Elizabeth shrugged off the vicar's minor scolding and replaced the teapot on the table. "It sounds like a splendid affair," he lied.

Elizabeth's eyes narrowed suspiciously, but he smiled warmly back at her. "Am I right in assuming that His Grace is none other than my old friend the duke of Welford?"

Elizabeth nodded reluctantly.

"I must call on him while I am here," he said

smoothly. "Perhaps I might manage an invitation to this party also."

"But you wouldn't know anyone there," Margaret protested.

"But I know you," he reminded her with a gentle smile.

Margaret fell back in her chair, biting her bottom lip nervously, while Mr. Crewe stood up impatiently.

"My duties await me, and I must not overstay my welcome," he announced with a pointed look at Alex.

Margaret and Elizabeth also rose to their feet. "It was so kind of you to call on us, Lord Waring," Elizabeth said. "You must give our best regards to your father."

There was little Alex could do but prepare to leave also. "That sounds almost as if I am not welcome here any longer," he teased. Suspecting that Elizabeth would agree, he turned to look sadly at Margaret.

"You must feel free to come at any time," she assured him halfheartedly.

When the door closed after the two men, Elizabeth turned to her mother. "What could ever have possessed him to come here?" she wondered suspiciously.

Margaret sank to her chair, her hands lying limply in her lap. "You don't think he really was just passing through town?" she asked her daughter hopefully.

"No, I don't," she said quickly. "Nor did I trust all his pleasant smiles and easy manners. He reminds me too much of his father for me to be delighted to see him."

"But, Libby," Margaret pointed out, "you only met his father once."

Elizabeth nodded grimly as she sat down next to her mother and took one of her hands. "Yes, and that once was enough to make me detest him forever!" She stood up and walked over to the window to stare out at Ben working in the garden.

Elizabeth could remember the duke's one visit all too clearly. It had been a few weeks after her father had died, and she had been painfully aware of their precarious financial position. Foolishly, she had been delighted to see His Grace, believing that he had come to help them. After a few minutes in his presence, she was no longer pleased. He had been domineering and overbearing, and her mother had spent his whole visit quivering in silent apprehension.

As thin as a scarecrow in her cheap black mourning dress, Elizabeth had known that she looked a fright, but she had not cared. Holding tightly to her mother's trembling hand, she had faced the duke squarely, answering all his questions in a cold, forbidding voice. Although the house was too shabby for words and their clothes were obviously cheaply made, he had not asked them if they needed anything. He had stayed for a few hours, then abruptly taken his leave. Whether he had come out of duty after his cousin's death or because he was merely curious about them, Elizabeth never learned, for they had not heard from him again; but she was not inclined to trust his son.

Margaret stood up. "What makes you so certain that he is here for a reason?" she asked.

Giving her mother a wry look, Elizabeth shook her head. "I doubt that he was so lonely that he decided to search for his distant cousins."

"I suppose not," Margaret agreed.

Elizabeth continued, barely aware that her mother had spoken. "Neither he nor his father has ever felt the need to improve our relationship, so why would he suddenly appear now? What can we have that he wants?"

Margaret paled slightly. "Maybe it has nothing to do with us," she suggested.

"Of course it must," Elizabeth said, shaking her head slowly. "They've ignored us for years; now suddenly my charming cousin comes to visit. It must have something to do with us, but I'll wager that we won't be the ones who profit from this visit. No, Lord Waring was quite determined. I was completely rude to him, but he appeared not to notice. Either he's a dreadful slowtop or he's willing to ignore a great deal until he achieves his goal."

"What goal?" Margaret asked.

Elizabeth shrugged and rubbed her forehead absently. "There ought to be a way to make him so uncomfortable that he can't stay."

Shaking her head in confusion, Margaret began to pile the dishes from their tea onto a cart near the door. She had just finished wiping up a few drops of spilled tea when Elizabeth stood up with a happy cry.

"What's wrong?"

Elizabeth smiled. "Why, nothing at all," she said. The twinkle of laughter in her eyes made her look totally different from the grim young lady Alex had just faced. "If our dear cousin wants to visit us again, I shall be most happy to see him. In fact, I will eagerly await his every visit for the excitement it brings into my dull little life."

Margaret just stared at her. "What are you talking about?"

Grinning outrageously, Elizabeth ran lightly across the floor and swung the last of the dishes from her mother's hands. "What could possibly make him take flight sooner than if his plain spinster cousin falls madly in love with him?"

Morgana was definitely not in the mood for *Julius Caesar*. The only reason she had agreed to attend was the fact that it was one of the last theatrical performances before the end of the season, and since Alex had left town, time was weighing rather heavily on her hands.

It was not as if Alex were her only admirer. She had numerous others just waiting for some sign that she was tiring of him. There was no hope that she would, of course, but it was pleasant to have a few adoring slaves about.

She smiled at the man sitting next to her. Sir Quentin Paine was certainly nothing like Alex. He was older, in his forties, with graying hair, and although he dressed with good taste, there was little he could do to conceal his protruding waistline. But he was extremely fond of her and tended to be astonishingly generous when she granted him the slightest favor. If she had never met Alex and had not aspired to move in his elite circle of society, she probably could have overlooked Sir Quentin's small vulgarities and the hints of his unscrupulous past. As it was, she was content to use him as an occasional escort and keep her eyes set on far better prey.

"I fear this just isn't my style, my dear." Sir Quentin laughed as the curtain was pulled across the stage after the first act. "Too deadly serious for me."

Morgana shrugged. It was not to her taste, either, but she did not feel particularly agreeable this evening. Alex appeared to have gone to the country to sulk after the argument with his father, and he had not even thought to invite her along.

"Why don't we take a stroll in the halls and see who's about?" Sir Quentin suggested. Morgana followed silently.

"Although you do look fetching when you pout, you really should not let Waring drive you to a fit of sullens," Sir Quentin told her quietly as they stepped out into the hall.

"He has nothing to do with it," Morgana protested. "And if you find my company so lacking—" She stopped suddenly and with a sensuous toss of her vibrant hair smiled warmly at the man coming toward them. Alex's father was just the person she longed to see.

"Why, Your Grace," she purred. Her shawl slipped down her arm, exposing the smooth white skin of her shoulder. "How marvelous to see you."

The duke nodded coldly, appearing rather forbidding in his formal black and white attire. She stayed determinedly in his way, even though he moved slightly trying to get around her.

"I do hope that you have recovered from your terrible experience the other day," she said with obvious concern.

"Experience?" he snapped, wishing she would let him pass. His highly polished boots tapped impatiently on the floor.

"Oh, yes," she laughed lightly. "Alex said you had quite a shock the other day when you found out you could no longer order him about as if he were a child."

His Grace glared at her with a murderous look before he pushed past her, but she only laughed. Turning around to watch him leave, she called out, "Would you like me to give Alex a message for you?" She laughed even louder.

"I would say he is not one of your most ardent

admirers," Sir Quentin said quietly when His Grace was no longer in sight.

Morgana shrugged. "I have the feeling that the only thing he ardently admires is his money. That, and his good name," she added with a laugh.

Sir Quentin took her arm and they began to walk further down the hallway. "I don't know about that," he said thoughtfully. "He was quite sought after when I first came to London, but he never showed any interest in marrying again. Apparently he was one of those fools who want no other woman once the one they loved is gone."

Morgana looked skeptical. "So his wife died. That doesn't mean he should begrudge others the chance to enjoy love. Besides," she added, "I doubt he's capable of really loving someone."

Sir Quentin raised his eyebrows in surprise. "You really hate him, don't you."

Morgana stopped walking and turned to him. "I have no time in my life for hate," she said with a secret smile. Her fingers gently tugged at his cravat, and he looked down at her thoughtfully.

"Why do you stay with Waring?" he asked. "You deserve more than he's willing to give you. Let me show you how I appreciate you."

Morgana smiled but shook her head. "And how do you know what he's willing to give?"

"Lady Tremayne."

Morgana turned about impatiently to see one of

her footmen hurrying toward her. "What are you doing here?" she snapped.

"A message cum fer ya," the man told her. "It were importent, so aye came right here." He held out a small piece of paper sealed with a large piece of wax.

Morgana took the paper and glanced toward Sir Quentin. He took her arm and moved her to the side of the hallway. There was nowhere they could go for privacy, but a branch of candles was on the wall nearby, and it was fairly light.

Ripping open the paper, Morgana read through the message quickly. The footman gaped at the crowd with interest, while Sir Quentin watched Morgana's face.

"It's not bad news, is it?" he asked when she looked up.

She turned to him, having forgotten for a moment that he was there. "Bad news?" she repeated, then laughed. "Oh no, it's the best news ever." She folded the paper carefully and tucked it into her reticule. "Francis has died, and his timing could not have been better. Alex will be delighted when I send him word."

In the middle of the next morning, before Elizabeth had even finished her chores, Bertha came to tell her that Alex had called.

She thanked Bertha quietly, putting just a hint of excitement into her voice, and took off the large white apron that covered her dark green day dress. Her hands trembled slightly with anticipation as she smoothed down her skirt and patted her hair into place. The housekeeper smiled kindly at her, thinking that it was high time Miss Libby had a handsome gentleman caller.

Elizabeth, though, was anxious only for the chance to pit her wits against those of this pompous fool. She had bested his father, and she was going to do the same with the son. She would show him up to be the gudgeon he was!

She hurried into the parlor and stopped shyly just inside the door, delighted that she looked her worst.

"I've come to take you for a drive," Alex told her with a disarming smile.

Elizabeth smiled back uncertainly, silently giving him credit for not showing dismay at her appearance. "Have you a carriage?" she asked as she walked across the parlor to look out the window. A gleaming black curricle trimmed with silver stood before the house. Two beautiful gray horses stood restlessly waiting as Ben looked them over approvingly. Elizabeth turned back to Alex. It required little effort on her part to light her eyes with excitement, but she fought hard to remain demure. "Is that yours?" she whispered. "Oh, yes. I should so love to go for a ride in it."

Alex laughed indulgently as her hands covered her blushing cheeks. "It will just take me a moment to tidy myself," she promised him, and seemingly embarrassed by her display of excitement, she hurried from the room.

After closing the door behind her, Elizabeth stood quietly in the hallway, listening at the parlor door. She heard Alex take a few steps. He must have turned to her mother, who had been quietly embroidering across the room. Elizabeth could picture her sitting there in her pale rose dress with her hair neatly tucked up under a lace cap with matching rose ribbons. She could also picture her worried expression and hoped her mother would play along, for she had had some misgivings about the idea.

"And what about you?" she heard Alex tease. "Shall I take you for a ride also?"

"Oh, no," Margaret sighed. "But it will be such a treat for Libby. She so rarely has any fun."

Elizabeth could just imagine Alex nodding in agreement about their dreary lives. She ran up the stairs quickly before she burst into laughter.

It only took her a moment to pull her hair back even tighter and put on an old lace cap of her mother's. She threw a black shawl over her shoulders and winced as she passed the mirror opposite her bedroom door. She looked positively dreadful!

Alex, however, smiled approvingly at her as she entered the room. "Are you ready for your ride?" He reached over to take her hand.

Margaret gave Elizabeth a worried glance and rose to her feet as the two walked toward the door. "Have a pleasant ride," she said nervously and smiled at them weakly as they left the house.

"I've never ridden in one of these before," Elizabeth confided as she was handed up in the curricle. She looked around her with interest, but remembered herself as Alex climbed up next to her. She swallowed nervously a few times, glancing at the ground, and tightly clutched the edge of the seat.

"I'm honored that you trust my driving skill." His voice was soft and reassuring as he flicked the reins, and the horses pulled the carriage away from the house.

Elizabeth smiled at him. "Actually you are the only one who ever asked me," she confided quietly.

An old woman walking along the side of the road waved to them as they tooled along. Elizabeth longed to wave back and shout hello, but she was determined to play her part to the hilt. She would be a simpering, die-away miss, totally enamored of her handsome cousin until he cried off and left town.

Occasionally she glanced at him with a fond little smile, pretending to be more aware of him than of the scenery they were passing. Strangely enough, he did not seem to be bothered by her behavior and would smile back at her.

They rode in silence into the center of town. There were a few people about, but no one came too near the carriage. A dog ran out from behind the inn and darted into the middle of the street. Although it was not dangerously close to them, Elizabeth gasped in fear and tightly clutched the edge of the seat as Alex easily drove around the animal.

"You drive so well," she sighed, seeming enormously relieved that they had not hit the dog. "You must drive through crowds often."

Since the street was almost empty, she thought he might be slightly suspicious of her sincerity, but he just nodded solemnly. "Yes, but we were lucky, for I wasn't really concentrating. Having you here next to me is quite distracting."

Elizabeth bowed her head to hide the confusion that his remark was intended to cause and tried hard not to laugh. Did he really think she would believe such outrageous remarks?

They passed some children in the churchyard, who stared up at her in wonder. "We must give them something to appreciate," Alex said.

Without warning he flicked his whip over the heads of his horses and pulled on the reins. They turned in unison around the corner of the church and headed out of town, leaving behind a cloud of dust. As the country around them became more open, he allowed them to choose their own speed.

The wind was rushing through Elizabeth's hair, loosening it from its confining pins and putting color into her cheeks. It was a glorious feeling to be racing along the road, and she closed her eyes in sheer delight.

"You aren't frightened, are you?" he asked.

Elizabeth opened her eyes with a start and slowly shook her head. "Not with you," she said bravely.

Alex rewarded her with another smile and patted her hand gently. Luckily, going at such a speed required all his attention, and Elizabeth did not have to pretend nervousness for long. As he watched ahead of them, she lost herself in the thrill of the ride.

All too soon they turned around and headed back toward town. Elizabeth forced herself to smile sweetly at him. "I imagine our little village must seem quite dull to someone like yourself who lives in London all the time," she sighed.

He smiled at her fondly. "No, it seems quite peaceful to me. After all the noise and confusion of London, I truly enjoy being in the country. I have one home in Devonshire that reminds me very much of the area around Welford."

"But I imagine you must be far too busy to go there much," Elizabeth continued. "How lucky we are that you can spare time for us."

"No, I am the lucky one to have found such relations as you and your mother," he said, his voice sounding sincere.

Under the pretense of embarrassment, Elizabeth looked away, but now she was annoyed. At least he should be made uneasy by her enraptured attention, but he was acting as if it delighted him! He was the most provoking person she had ever met. Much worse than his father.

* * *

"Well," Margaret demanded as soon as they were alone in the parlor, "is he leaving soon?"

Elizabeth took off her shawl and sat down. "No," she said crossly. "Not yet."

Margaret's forehead creased with worry, and her face looked pale. "Why not? Wasn't he fooled by your plan?"

Elizabeth shook her head in puzzlement. "I vowed, ogled and simpered until I was nauseated, but he didn't seem at all upset."

Sinking down on a small footstool next to Elizabeth, Margaret clutched the arm of her daughter's chair tightly. "What will you do now?"

Elizabeth looked surprised at the question, and picking up her shawl, she laughed. "Oh, I'm not giving up," she assured Margaret. "I'll find some perfect way to embarrass him with my attentions at dinner."

"Dinner?"

"Oh, yes, I begged him to come to dinner tonight," she said as she stood up. "That gives me a few hours to decide just how I'll throw myself at him. By tomorrow afternoon he will be far from Welford."

"Oh, Libby, I wish I could be certain of that," her mother breathed fervently.

Elizabeth laughed again and, bending down, kissed her mother's hair lightly. "Even if he isn't, what can he do to us? He could move into the Golden Boar, and although it might be annoying, we aren't really in danger from him." She smiled reassuringly as she left the room.

Margaret listened for a moment to her daughter's footsteps as they ascended the stairs. "I wish you were right, Libby," she whispered desperately to herself.

CHAPTER FOUR

Alex sighed impatiently as he looked out the window for the fifth time. He had ordered a carriage brought around for him at two o'clock so that he could escort Elizabeth and her mother to the garden party, but it appeared that no one in this fool place could read a clock.

He stalked out of the private parlor and went to the front door of the inn. The courtyard was empty.

"Blast!" he muttered. "I shall be late!" Today was an especially inconvenient day to be late, for he had decided that this farce of a courtship had gone on long enough. It was time to propose.

Turning to go back into the inn, he stopped as he saw a newspaper lying on a bench along the inn wall. He picked it up and sat down, noting with surprise that it was a recent edition.

There were rumors that Napoleon was trying to raise another army, the Prince Regent was asking Parliament to increase his allowance and two men in a balloon had ascended from Hyde Park and traveled four miles outside London.

Nothing was new, he thought as he folded the paper and tapped it against his knee. He glared in the direction of the stables and was about to stand up when, glancing down, a small item in the newspaper caught his eye.

Sir Francis Tremayne had died in his country home. The article noted the presence of his six daughters at his deathbed but did not mention his wife.

That should curtail Morgana's activities for a while, he said to himself with a laugh as he tossed the paper aside. Although, knowing Morgana, he could not imagine her going into mourning for even a few months. Certainly not for a whole year.

The clatter of horses signaled the arrival of his carriage, and Alex stood up, already having forgotten the news of Sir Francis's death as he planned his strategy for the day. After climbing up into the carriage, he directed the coachman to drive quickly to the Corbett house.

"We shall be the envy of all the ladies there," Elizabeth sighed when she saw his magnificent dark green coat and light tan breeches.

He shook his head with a smile. "No, I shall be envied by all the men, for who could ask for two lovelier companions," he said, trying to look approvingly at her. She was wearing a hideous lavender dress that made her pale skin look positively deathly.

Why didn't someone take the stupid chit in hand and teach her how to dress? He turned to Margaret in relief.

"You look lovely, as always," he told her, finding her gray dress a bit too somber for his taste but at least a flattering style and color.

Margaret said nothing, only smiling nervously at him while she picked up her reticule and shawl.

"I was so surprised that you managed an invitation so easily," Elizabeth murmured as they entered the carriage.

"As it happens, the duke and I are old friends. He was only too happy to invite me."

Elizabeth tried to look impressed. "Just think! You are friends of a duke," she cried in awe.

Margaret was suddenly overcome, coughing fitfully into her handkerchief.

"Are you all right?" Alex asked in concern.

Margaret nodded, still unable to speak, but Elizabeth saw the amusement in her mother's eyes. "It's the excitement of the party," she confided to Alex as she patted her mother's hand gently. "It's the high point of her life."

As Margaret began to cough again, Alex reached over to pat her hand also. "You must try to relax," he told her kindly. "You don't want to make yourself too ill to attend."

By the time they pulled into Welford Park, Margaret was her quiet self again. Aside from a definite glare at her daughter, she appeared to suffer no ill affects from her excitement.

Welford Park was not very large by London standards. Many country estates of lesser title were far bigger, but in the eyes of the village's inhabitants, it was quite grand.

A wide carriageway led from the road to the house. About halfway there it split and formed a graceful loop that passed directly by the elegant entrance. On either side of the drive were thick, luscious lawns, while in the circle of lawn surrounded by the drive there was a graceful fountain surrounded by a rose garden.

To the west side of the house, under the shade of several tall trees, tables of food had been set up. Smaller tables with chairs were scattered nearby for the guests to eat at.

"Oh, isn't it all splendid?" Elizabeth sighed dramatically as Alex took her arm.

"It's fine enough, I suppose," he said, "but I much prefer either of my estates."

Elizabeth turned to him in wonder. "You mean they are lovelier than this?" she asked.

"Much," he laughed. God, she was ridiculously easy to impress!

Once they had greeted their host and hostess, Margaret wandered off to join some friends. Several people came to speak to Elizabeth, but Alex did not allow her to linger with them.

"I daresay my friends are just too dull for you,"

she said with a sigh after he had maneuvered them away from two young ladies.

Since those two were so busy trying to impress him that they barely spoke to her at all, he wondered how she could call them her friends. "I imagine your friends are all fascinating," he lied smoothly, "but I don't want to share you with anyone."

Of course that made Elizabeth blush and giggle, and he was able to steer her toward the tables of food, where there were few people at the moment.

A footman held plates for them both while Alex chose which of the delectable dishes they would sample. Elizabeth, as he had expected, was of no help. Either she had no opinions or was willing to bow to his superior judgment.

Alex leaned over a plate of marinated fish, trying to decide if the peculiar smell he detected was coming from them. He decided to skip those and was about to tell the footman to give them some of the fresh strawberries in another bowl when he became aware of a voice behind him. Turning quickly, he found Mr. Crewe involved in a somewhat heated argument with his cousin.

"It's not like you to be so rude," the vicar scolded Elizabeth. "The children did so want to say hello to you, yet you passed them without a word."

"I didn't see them," she said impatiently. "You make it sound as if I deliberately snubbed them. They were nowhere near me."

"How wonderful to see you again," Alex said to

Mr. Crewe, then turned to his cousin. "You do like strawberries, don't you? Or would you prefer a peach?"

Elizabeth looked uneasily at the vicar before turning to Alex. She shrugged her shoulders. "Oh, I don't . . ."

"Elizabeth is coming with me to greet my family," Mr. Crewe said officiously as he took her arm.

Alex was equally quick to take her other arm. "But we were just getting something to eat." His eyes pleaded with Elizabeth. "Surely you wouldn't leave me by myself. I don't know anyone else here."

Mr. Crewe spotted two young ladies a few feet away, whispering and giggling as they openly ogled His Lordship. "I am certain that you will find someone to keep you company. Come along now, Elizabeth," he ordered.

"May I take these to your table, my lord?" the footman asked.

As Alex turned to him in surprise, his hand let go of Elizabeth's arm. By the time he had turned back to her, she was gone.

"Blast!" he muttered to himself. The footman stood impassively nearby. "You may as well see if you can find me a table," Alex said to him in disgust.

Alex followed the footman across the lawn toward an empty table in the midst of many filled ones. Alex, however, spotted an empty one on the edge, slightly away from the others.

"Take the plates over there," he ordered. He

would give Crewe a few minutes, then he would retrieve Elizabeth.

A hand on his shoulder interrupted his thoughts. He turned to find a stout, gray-haired man beaming at him.

"Aren't you Alex Waring?" he cried. "My boy Willard was at Eton with you. You must remember him—Willard Atkinson?"

He continued to smile expectantly, but Alex just stared at him dumbly. Who the devil was this fellow?

"Oh, the things he used to tell me about you!" The man began to chuckle heartily. "And the trouble you two would get into! Better not try any of it now," he laughed. "I'm the local magistrate, and I'd hate to have to come out to your lovely cousins' house to do my arresting."

As Alex continued to stare at him, the older man reached down and took Alex's hand, shaking it firmly. "I can hardly wait to tell Willard that I saw you. He'll think I'm bamming him." Leaning closer to Alex, he whispered confidentially, "He avoids these affairs like the devil! Says they're too flat for him. He'll never believe you actually came here." He pounded Alex on the back. "Well, good to see you, my boy! You must drop in and see us when you are in the neighborhood." With that he took himself off.

Alex stared after him for a few moments in total bewilderment. Then he shook his head sharply and looked around for Elizabeth. He frowned when he saw her firmly ensconced among the vicar's children.

Well, he was not about to let some bird-witted ninnyhammer spoil his plans now that he had gotten this far. His lips tightened with determination as he marched over to where they all stood, laughing and talking.

Actually, though, he did not have to fight anyone to get her back. As he approached, he saw a little old lady hurry over to speak to Elizabeth. After she left, Elizabeth herself left the vicar and his family and, with a quick glance around the lawn, hurried over to where he stood.

"Mother's gone," she told him with a worried frown.

"You mean she left the party?" he asked, vaguely aware that she seemed different from the adoring old maid she had been earlier.

Elizabeth nodded. "Mrs. Lane came to tell me she has gone home." It was obvious that she was really concerned.

Taking her arm, Alex led her back over to the table he had found for them so that they would be away from the others. "Was she ill?" he asked. "She was upset in the carriage coming here," he reminded her.

"Oh, that." Elizabeth dismissed the incident with a shake of her head. "No, Mrs. Lane said she wasn't ill, that she just wanted to leave."

"Perhaps there was something else she had to do," he suggested. "Or someone was here whom she preferred not to see."

Elizabeth shook her head again. Except for him, there was no one here her mother would want to avoid.

"We can leave, too, if it will make you feel better," he suggested, kindly patting her hand.

"Do you mind?" she asked quickly.

He stood up with a smile. "I only came here to be with you," he reminded her.

She stood up also, meeting his smile uneasily. Somehow her plan to embarrass him had never quite succeeded.

Alex sent a footman to call for their carriage and escorted Elizabeth toward the drive. He made a vague excuse for their early departure to His Grace and quickly helped her into the carriage.

"I am probably being silly," she told him as they pulled away from Welford Park. "Mother may have simply spilled something on her dress and wanted to leave quietly."

Alex smiled at her, but his mind was not really on what she was saying. This was the very opportunity he had been waiting for, he realized. Suddenly leaning forward, he took her hand in his.

"This may be the wrong time to tell you this," he said quickly, "but my heart can no longer contain itself."

Elizabeth turned to stare at him, her eyes wide with surprise. She looked rather stunned, Alex thought.

Bending his head slightly to suggest earnest supplication but actually to hide his laughter, Alex tightened his hold on her hand. "Surely you must realize how I feel about you, for I've worn my heart for all to see." He peeked up at her. She was quite pale. "I never dreamed I would find someone as wonderful as you."

"Oh, Alex," Elizabeth cried distractedly as she tried to pull her hand free.

He grabbed her other hand, too, and holding them both tightly, he brought them up to his lips. First sprinkling little kisses along her fingers, he soon turned her hands over and kissed the inside of her wrists. "At first you were so cold to me that I was in despair, but then you changed, and I could see that you returned my feelings."

"Alex!" Elizabeth gasped. She had given up on her hands and tried instead to edge away from him. "Please . . . you mustn't say such things."

"No, you're right," he agreed too easily. "We have no need for words." Without warning, he scooped her into his arms, and his lips came down firmly on hers.

Elizabeth squirmed frantically in his arms, trying to push him away, but he merely attributed her efforts to maidenly shyness. Raining light kisses along her cheek, he pushed her gently back against the soft velvet squabs of the carriage.

"Alex, please," she whispered pleadingly as his fingers loosened her tightly pinned hair. "You mustn't."

He pulled back slightly, smiling down into her watery eyes. Good Lord, he laughed to himself, the chit was horrified! Hadn't she ever been kissed before?

"You can't deny that you care for me," he continued ruthlessly. "Your eyes have told me the truth." He picked up her hand again, realizing it was safer not to look directly at her. Instead he began to kiss the tip of each finger.

"Alex, please, this is awful," Elizabeth cried, sounding close to tears. "I never meant . . . I never thought . . ." She gulped in despair.

"I know," he agreed wickedly. "You never thought we could be so happy. It's like a dream come true."

"That's not . . ." The carriage came to a sudden halt in front of the Corbett house.

Blast, Alex thought, my timing is off. He grabbed her hands in desperation. "Tell me you'll marry me," he pleaded. "I won't let you go until you agree." He felt the coachman jump down and hoped that Elizabeth would not test the seriousness of his remark.

"Oh, Alex, I can't," she cried, pulling her hands away from him.

The devil! What sort of game was she playing at now? "You don't mean that," he argued. He felt a moment's panic. Had he proposed too soon?

The coachman opened the door, and Elizabeth practically stumbled in her desire to get out. Alex quickly jumped down after her and took her hand.

"I shan't come in," he told her softly. "You will want to talk to your mother alone, but I shall return after dinner. Then we can make plans." He lifted her hand to his lips and kissed it slowly, letting his lips linger on her skin.

Elizabeth blushed a vivid red and pulled her hand back as quickly as she could. She would have liked to tell him not to come again, but she didn't have the courage to be so rude. Besides, he had jumped back into the carriage and was already gone.

Feeling totally despicable, Elizabeth trudged toward the house. Because she had been so suspicious of Alex when he came, she had set out deliberately to trick him and, instead, had totally misjudged him. Instead of accepting his honest offer of friendship, she had continued to mistrust him, cruelly planning to humiliate him, for no other reason than that she disliked his father! She was aware that she was abysmally ignorant about men, but common decency should have kept her from being so malicious.

Elizabeth let herself into the house quietly, hoping that she could slip up to her room unnoticed. She needed time to collect her thoughts and decide what she would say to Alex that night. But as the door closed behind her, the parlor door opened and her mother rushed out.

"Oh, Elizabeth, I must speak with you," Margaret cried, then promptly burst into tears.

With a sigh Elizabeth pushed back a heavy section of hair that Alex had loosened and led her mother back into the parlor. She pushed her gently down onto the sofa and sat down next to her.

"Now tell me what's wrong," she urged.

Margaret tried hard to stop the flow of tears, but it was some time before she was coherent enough to speak. "You've got to help me," she finally managed to say.

"Of course," Elizabeth soothed. "Just tell me what you want me to do."

Wiping her eyes with a small, soggy square of linen, Margaret took a deep breath, then turned to face her daughter. "It's about Alex," she said quickly, but did not notice Elizabeth's sudden paling. "I know why he's here."

"You do?" Elizabeth's voice was a hoarse whisper.

Margaret nodded, and wiped away a few stray tears on one cheek. "He's come for the necklace."

"The necklace?"

Looking up at her daughter, Margaret tried to smile. "The Herriad Necklace," she said. "You probably don't even remember it. I can't say when I had it out last, but I do still have it tucked away on my closet shelf, and now they want it back."

"Do you mean that diamond necklace?" she whispered fearfully.

Her mother nodded and tried to smile again.

"It's not yours?"

The smile disappeared as she shook her head.

"Then why did you have it all these years?" Elizabeth asked in confusion, a dreadful fear growing inside her.

Margaret's eyes filled with tears again, and she valiantly tried to blink them away. "You see . . . it's because . . ." She gulped suddenly. "I stole it."

Elizabeth fell back in her chair and stared at her mother. She felt as if she had somehow stumbled into a bad dream but had no hope of waking up soon. She knew her mouth was opening and closing, but no sound was coming out.

"I didn't mean to steal it," Margaret assured her hesitantly. "I didn't even know I had until it was too late, and then your father said we'd have to keep it or Gerald would send me to prison."

"Gerald?" Elizabeth's voice was weak.

"Alex's father. It really belongs to him."

"How did you ever get a necklace that belonged to him?" Elizabeth whispered hoarsely.

Margaret wrung her hands together. "You see, my parents died when I was very young, and I had no other relatives. My godmother, who was also Gerald's aunt, sent me to school, and then when I was almost seventeen, she brought me to live with her. I had no experience with society or men, but she was going to present me during the next London season." Margaret glanced up at her daughter, hoping that Elizabeth would have lost interest, but she hadn't.

"Before the season began," Margaret continued, "we were invited to stay with Gerald at his home in the country. He was having a house party and wanted his aunt to act as his hostess, since his wife was dead. Once the party was over, there were only a few weeks before the season was due to start, so Gerald persuaded my godmother that we should stay on at his house and go to London from there."

"So you stole the necklace while you were at his house?" Elizabeth asked in bewilderment.

"Oh, no," her mother cried, horrified. "He often let his aunt wear the family jewelry, and he let me wear the Herriad Necklace for a special party he was giving." Margaret stopped speaking and sat staring into the empty fireplace. Elizabeth could hear Bertha moving around in the kitchen and hoped she would not disturb them with tea.

"Did you meet Father through your godmother, too?" she asked her mother.

Margaret started slightly, then nodded. "He lived with Gerald, although they never got along. I think Gerald felt it was his obligation to provide for Timothy, but your father resented everything that anyone tried to do for him. Gerald was his cousin, and only a few years older than him, but they were so different. Timothy was always laughing and playing, while Gerald seemed so settled, with the estates to run and Alex still in the nursery." She sighed and lapsed into silence again.

"And the necklace?" Elizabeth prompted.

"Oh." Margaret jumped slightly. "I was wearing

it the night of the party, and your father and I eloped."

"You eloped?" Elizabeth squeaked.

Margaret had not even heard her. "I didn't even realize I had it on until we were far from home. I wanted to send it back, but your father said it was too late. Gerald would never forgive me."

"But if you had lived in his house, surely he wouldn't have done anything to you," Elizabeth tried to reason.

Margaret looked at her daughter, her eyes wide with fear. "He was a very hard man and could not forgive anyone. He had found your father and me together in the garden." Margaret closed her eyes tightly and Elizabeth noticed how pale she was. "It was nothing, really, but Gerald was very angry. He said terrible things to me. I didn't know what to do. Nothing had prepared me for such a situation. But I did know I could not stay there with him hating me so and obviously regretting any kindness that he had shown me. When Timothy asked me to elope with him, I agreed. It was the perfect way to relieve my godmother of my bothersome presence and to free Gerald from a situation that had become quite embarrassing to him."

"But that was such a long time ago. You don't know that he's still angry at you."

Margaret shook her head. "You saw him when he came here after your father's death. He still hated me then, and it was sixteen years since I had seen him."

Elizabeth could understand her mother's fear. She sighed and looked over at her, rubbing her forehead wearily. "But what makes you think that Alex has come for the necklace? Has he asked you for it?"

"No." Margaret shook her head. "He's sending the magistrate out here for me." She sniffed as a few tears ran down her cheeks.

"Mr. Atkinson? How do you know that? Why didn't he just ask you for it?"

"They were talking at the party, and I overheard Mr. Atkinson say he was coming here to arrest me," Margaret cried. "But I thought . . . since you seem to know Alex so well . . . and he seems to be fond of you . . . that maybe you could just ask him to take it back."

Oh no, Elizabeth thought. With the shock of learning that the necklace was stolen, she had forgotten the use she had been making of the stones!

Elizabeth turned to look at her mother, only to find her smiling hopefully at her. "He could take it and leave, and we . . . I would be safe," she said eagerly.

Yes, her mother would be safe until they took a good look at the stones in the necklace, Elizabeth realized numbly.

"Will you do it?" Margaret asked eagerly. "Will you give it back to Alex?"

Elizabeth stood up and walked across the room slowly. "Are you certain that's what he wants?" she asked. "Maybe he's here for something totally different."

"Oh, Libby, I wish it were true," Margaret sighed. "I've been trying to think of some other reason the whole time he's been here, but there just isn't another."

Elizabeth turned around and looked at her mother, trying to find a way to tell her about the paste stones. But each time she tried to speak, no words would come.

"I have been expecting them to ask for it back for years now," her mother went on. "That's why I thought Gerald had come before."

"Then how can you be so certain now?" Elizabeth's voice could barely be heard.

Margaret shrugged. "Look at Alex. He's a young man and probably ready to marry. He wants to give the necklace to his bride."

Elizabeth felt such a surge of relief course through her that her knees felt unable to support her. She did not bother to correct her mother, for she had suddenly seen the answer to her problem. "His wife!" she cried. "Of course, his wife will get it!"

Margaret just stared at her as Elizabeth hurried across the room and sat down next to her mother. She picked up her mother's hands and held them tightly. "Don't you see? It's going to be all right!" she cried again, tears forming in her eyes. "His wife will get the necklace, and that will be me, because today he asked me to marry him!"

CHAPTER FIVE

The carriage rocked wildly back and forth as the wheels seemed to find every hole in the road. Elizabeth clung to the strap on the wall, trying not to lose her balance. Every part of her body ached, and the moment the carriage stopped, she felt, she would probably fall asleep from exhaustion.

Just when she was certain she could endure no more, the carriage slowed and turned. The bumping and jolting ceased. Elizabeth peered at the landscape they were passing but could see nothing but neat rows of trees that lined whatever road they were on. At any rate, it was a relief not to be so tossed about.

Letting go of the strap, she fell back against the side of the carriage and sighed. It was hard to believe that she had married Alex two days ago and was now on her way to his country home, Herriaton. She certainly hoped they would arrive soon, for she was quite weary of traveling.

After what seemed like several more miles, the carriage slowed to a halt. She heard Alex giving instructions to someone; then the coachman pulled open the door, and she climbed stiffly out. They were at the foot of a massive flight of stairs leading to the entrance to the largest house she had ever seen. It seemed to stretch in an endless line along the avenue. She looked up the stairs and saw two footmen hurrying down toward them.

Looking about her nervously, she found Alex at her elbow. "Is this your home?" she asked in amazement.

He said nothing in reply, merely taking her arm and leading her toward the stairs.

Elizabeth did not bother to repeat her question, for Alex had changed considerably in the last few days. He was no longer the charming companion he had been in Welford but was now cold and remote, as if he had become everything she had suspected him of earlier. Worry over her own problems with the necklace and the strain of traveling had made her too tired to care. She turned away from Alex, not wanting to notice that his eyes were glittery and hard, that his smile seemed strangely triumphant. He looked as cold and cruel as she remembered his father had been.

The stairway divided in half after about twenty steps, and each half twisted away toward the porticoed entrance. On her own Elizabeth would have stood undecided, hesitating over which side to use, but Alex just turned to the right and kept her moving with him.

The actual entrance to the house was not visible from the carriage level but soon came into sight. A wide stone overhang sheltered the two massive doors, which stood open. On either side of them stood two more footmen. A butler waited at the head of the stairs. The two footmen stood as statues, but the butler unbent slightly as they approached him. He bowed with the faintest of smiles.

"Welcome home, my lord," he said politely.

Alex nodded as he ushered Elizabeth past him into the house.

The foyer was huge, larger than any one room in Elizabeth's former home. The floor was a dark stone that made the room feel cool and unwelcoming as their footsteps rang out loudly. The walls were light and hung with portraits of grim-looking people; in one far corner a wide, curving staircase rose and disappeared into the shadows.

Alex led Elizabeth into the center of the room. She heard footsteps behind them, then the muffled sound of the doors being closed. The room was suddenly dim, the only light coming from windows high above where they stood. In spite of herself Elizabeth shivered and forced down the desire to run back to Welford.

Suddenly a door to their right swung open. Sunlight filtered into the foyer from the doorway, and a man stood silhouetted in the opening.

"I see you've returned," a chilling voice said.

Alex said nothing but tightened his hold on Elizabeth's arm and moved her across the foyer toward the open door. The man turned abruptly and went back into the room. Alex and Elizabeth followed him.

Just inside the room Alex let go of Elizabeth's arm and closed the door. She looked about her in wonder. They were in a library, and the walls from the floor to the ceiling far above her head were covered with books. Even the space above and below the two large windows was used to store books.

Alex came up next to her again and pulled her forward. His father, the man who had spoken earlier, was standing in the middle of the room. His expression was less than friendly, but Alex did not appear to notice.

"You remember our cousin Elizabeth, don't you?" Alex asked as he let go of her elbow and took her hand. "We wanted you to be among the first to wish us well." His father's eyes narrowed. "We were married two days ago." As he spoke Alex twisted her hand slightly so that the wide gold band that she wore was now visible.

His Grace said nothing for a moment, but he stared coldly at them both.

"I assume this is some sort of joke," he finally said, his voice showing how little humor he saw in the situation.

Rather than being cowed or even angered by his father's attitude, Alex began to laugh. "Why, Father, I thought you'd welcome my bride with open arms."

He put his arm around Elizabeth's shoulder and hugged her close, but there was no warmth in the gesture. She blushed furiously, suddenly conscious of how rough and shabby her clothes were compared to Alex's and his father's.

His Grace seemed to share her sentiments, for he looked her over slowly, from her dusty half-boots to her mussed hair. He turned away, but not before Elizabeth had seen the look of disgust on his face.

Standing before his desk with his back to them both, His Grace spoke. "If your 'bride' would be so kind," he said, putting a strange emphasis on the word, "I would like to speak to you alone."

With a careless shrug Alex walked over to a bell-pull and soundlessly tugged on it. Left alone in the middle of the room, Elizabeth felt vulnerable. She would have been grateful for the relative security of a chair, but no one suggested that she sit, and she was too nervous to take the initiative. She remained standing, twisting the long strap of her reticule around her hand, while Alex walked to his father's desk and idly flipped through a pile of correspondence.

A middle-aged woman dressed all in black knocked quietly and entered the room. She took no notice of Elizabeth but turned to His Grace.

"Mrs. Benson," Alex warmly greeted the housekeeper, "you are just the person we need. Elizabeth and I were married just a few days ago, and we've been traveling here ever since. Please show my wife to her room and make her comfortable," he said. "I'm sure she'd like a bite to eat, or at least a cup of tea."

The housekeeper's glance became more friendly. "Why, the poor dear." She shook her head sympathetically. "I'll fix her up just fine, my lord, don't you fret none." She walked over to the door and held it open. "If you'll come this way, my lady . . ."

Elizabeth looked over at Alex, reluctant to leave the only person she knew in this unfriendly place, but he ignored her silent plea, smiling blandly at her and waving his hand toward the door. She turned and followed the housekeeper out.

The door closed almost immediately behind them as they walked across the wide foyer toward the staircase.

"This is such a wonderful surprise," Mrs. Benson said quietly.

A loud burst of voices from the library could be heard over the echoing of their footsteps on the hard marble floor. Elizabeth blushed, but the housekeeper pretended not to notice.

They walked past some portraits in the foyer. One in particular caught Elizabeth's eye, for the woman depicted was wearing the Herriad Necklace.

"Who is that?" Elizabeth whispered, unable to take her eyes off the necklace. There was no doubt that it was the same one wrapped in a scrap of velvet and tucked into the corner of her trunk.

Mrs. Benson stopped and smiled fondly at the

picture. "That's the duchess," she said quietly. "Isn't she lovely?"

Elizabeth turned to her in surprise. "You mean his wife? Lord Waring's mother?"

Mrs. Benson nodded. "They were such a lovely couple. So devoted. It was such a tragedy that she died when Lord Waring was born." Elizabeth began to back away, but Mrs. Benson did not notice. "Do you see the necklace she is wearing?"

"Yes," Elizabeth gasped.

"It's been in the family for years, and it's given to the Herriad brides on the night of their betrothal. I 'spect they'll be getting it out for you."

"It's lovely," Elizabeth nodded weakly, then hurried away.

"There's a very nice room right next to his lordship," the housekeeper said, walking to the foot of the stairs. "Although once you're settled in, you may want to move to another part of the house."

As they started up the stairs, Elizabeth noticed the sound-muffling carpet with relief. She did not feel welcome here and preferred the feeling of invisibility that walking on the carpet gave her.

Her relief was short-lived, however, for as her footsteps became silent, other noises, especially the arguing in the library, became much louder.

"Damn it, Alex!" suddenly echoed through the room, "you have done some terrible things before, but I never believed you to be so despicable."

Elizabeth grew pale and did not dare look at the

housekeeper. Luckily they soon reached the top of the stairs and turned down a long hallway. If any more was said in the library, they could not hear it.

"Despicable?" Alex cried, glaring across the room at the other man. "You're the one who insisted that I marry!" he reminded him.

His father pounded his fist on the desk top. "Marry, yes, but not her!"

Alex smiled unpleasantly. "That's the real problem, isn't it? I took away your threatening power."

His Grace stared at his son for a long moment; then he sat down heavily. "That's all it is to you, isn't it? You have no feeling at all for that poor girl upstairs. She's just the perfect way to get your revenge. What has happened to you, Alex?" he snapped.

Alex ignored this last question as he, too, sat down. He stretched his legs out, ready to relax. "Oh, you can't fool me into thinking that you care a pittance about her," he said with a shake of his head. "You could barely suppress your dislike of her."

His Grace's lips tightened impatiently, and his hands twisted together in an effort to control his temper. "I admit I dislike her," he said tersely. "When I met her years ago, she was rude and overbearing—everything I dislike in a woman. She had her poor mother cowering nervously for fear of displeasing her. She was only fifteen at the time, but she ruled that household with an iron hand." He shook his head with disgust, then muttered, "That scheming hussy! She must have jumped at the chance to marry you!"

Alex sat up straighter and glared at his father irritably. "What makes you say that?"

"Are you that stupid!" His Grace cried. "She's got a title now and all your money to spend. God help you if she's inherited her father's gambling fever, though. I doubt that our entire fortune would last out the year!"

"Yet you were willing to leave your wealth to her if I hadn't married," Alex reminded him curtly.

"But I wouldn't have had to see it," his father pointed out. "She would not have had my name, so her scandalous behavior would not have shamed us all."

Alex jumped to his feet, his arms waving wide. "What are you talking about? What scandalous behavior?" he shouted. "You make her sound like a money-grubbing leech who has hidden her sinful past in order to entrap me!"

"And isn't that what she has done?" His father jumped to his feet also. "Do you think she married you for love?" he scoffed.

"Why not?" Alex said as he stood up and moved about the room, suddenly restless.

His father laughed scornfully. "Don't be an idiot! She kept her eye open for the main chance, and she certainly found it. Your wife!" he whispered hoarsely. "Didn't you notice how she was dressed? She has the manners of a parlor maid! Can you imagine what fools we'll look when you take her into society?"

"You're doing it too brown! One minute she's a gambling strumpet, and the next you make her sound like some innocent from a convent," Alex cried, stopping behind a gold damask chair, his hands clutching the back angrily. "Her manners are quite proper, there was no sign of any passion for gambling and I intend to burn all her clothes. She will do nothing to disgrace us."

"Nothing to disgrace us!" his father echoed incredulously. "She is a shrew and a termagant. Her father was a notorious gambler, and her mother a fool."

"Now just a moment," Alex cried, taking a step closer. "Margaret is a lovely, gentle woman. I won't have her brought into this argument."

"You won't?" his father shouted, even angrier now, if it were possible. "You know nothing about any of them. They ridiculed me publicly, made me look a fool. And you expect me to accept their daughter as your wife?"

Alex stared for a long, silent moment at his father. "It's not Elizabeth you hate," he said in quiet wonder. "It's them. You hate her parents. What happened? Did Cousin Timothy beat you in cards? Or did you just envy his charm?"

"Be quiet!" His Grace raged. "You cannot distract me with your idle speculation. The fact remains that you are married to a woman I find totally unacceptable. I only pray that it's not too late for an annulment, so that you can marry a woman you'd have a chance of happiness with."

His only answer was the slamming of the door behind his son.

Alex stormed up the stairs and turned down the hallway toward his rooms. He might have known that his father would not react predictably to the news of his marriage. He never was able to admit when he had been beaten.

As Alex passed the room next to his, the door opened and Elizabeth looked out. "Alex?" she called quietly.

With a sigh he turned his steps and entered the room. There was a tray of food and a pot of tea on a small table near the window. Although the food was untouched, one cup had been used. He took the other one, poured himself some tea and selected a cucumber sandwich from the plate.

He glanced up at her as he took a long drink of tea. She was standing a few feet away, watching him silently. He frowned when he saw that she was still wearing the same ugly dress in which she had been traveling. Her hair had been neatened, but it did not greatly help her appearance. The very sight of her brought back all his father's words, and he turned away from her in irritation, aware of a slight twinge of guilt. He walked over to the window and looked down at the rose garden below.

"He was very angry, wasn't he?" Elizabeth asked.

Alex glanced back at her. She was still holding her reticule like some damn guest. "No," he snapped. "He was delighted. Couldn't have been happier." He put the cup down on the table and turned back to the garden as if fascinated by the bright dots of color beneath him.

Elizabeth bit back an angry retort and forced her voice to be calm as she moved a step closer. "Did you know he would be?" she persisted.

Turning to face her, Alex's impatience was plain to see. "What is the point of going over it?" he asked. "So what if I suspected that he would not be pleased. What does it change?"

"It's my fault," she claimed as she sank wearily back into her chair. He stared at her questioningly. "I should have realized how he would feel, but I never gave him a thought."

"You mean you wouldn't have married me if you had known my father would not approve?" he asked skeptically.

She shook her head, her eyes cast downward on her nervously fidgeting hands. "I had no desire to come between you and your father, but I was very selfish and did not consider anyone else's feelings."

Alex stared at her bent head, his lips tightly compressed. The twinges of guilt had returned, a bit stronger this time, and they made him angry. "Oh, stop being such a martyr," he snapped. "It doesn't suit you!"

Elizabeth's eyes widened in surprise, but in this

strange, unfriendly place she did not have the spirit to argue. "I truly am sorry," she said with quiet firmness. "Perhaps if you told me just what he objects to, I could try to make myself more acceptable."

Not about to divulge his father's true objections, Alex shook his head impatiently. "For goodness' sake, you can't make yourself over for everyone. As soon as you changed one thing, he'd find something else to complain about. Just put him out of your mind and change for dinner." He turned to leave the room.

"But if I'm to live here with him . . ." she continued.

"You had better change for dinner," he said abruptly, and left the room.

Elizabeth stared at the closed door for several minutes, thoroughly discouraged. She had thought it was going to be so easy, that her only problem would be replacing the diamonds. She had never really considered that she would be married to Alex and supposedly making some sort of life with him. But how could she even talk to him when Alex had changed so? It seemed that just because of his father's disapproval, he was a totally different person. Well, she was not going to let that happen. "I'll show your father, Alex," she promised herself. "I'll make you the best wife possible, and one day he'll be glad that you married me."

Alex and his father were sitting in the parlor glaring at one another in silence when Elizabeth joined them for dinner. Alex could see that she had taken great pains with her appearance. She had chosen a dove gray dress that was probably her best, although it made her look like some damn governess. He looked away, irritated.

His Grace stood up at her entrance. "I believe dinner is waiting," he said impatiently, turning from the room. Alex took Elizabeth's arm and followed him to the dining room.

The room was huge, with ornate plasterwork on the upper walls and ceiling. On the walls hung a series of paintings depicting hunting scenes, from the beginning of the hunt to the killing and skinning of a deer and the roasting of it over an outdoor fire.

In the middle of the room stood a long table. Alex sat down at its foot, while his father sat at the head. Elizabeth was placed in the middle of one side, across from the painting showing the skinning of the deer.

The food was delicious, as it usually was at Herriaton, but no one said a word. Alex ate little and drank almost continuously, watching his father and Elizabeth with a brooding glare. His father only glanced his way once, then kept his eyes on his plate. Alex was tempted to carry on a flirtatious conversation with Elizabeth just to annoy his father, but she was too far away. Shouting was not conducive to romance.

When the meal was over at last, Elizabeth stood up uncertainly to leave the men to their port.

"I think I shall have mine in the parlor with Elizabeth," Alex announced, standing up also.

Elizabeth smiled gratefully at him, but his father glowered from the end of the table. "Gentlemen drink their port in the dining room," he bellowed.

Alex favored him with a smile, then poured himself a glass of port and quickly drank it down while he stood there.

"There, I've had my port," he said, and placed the glass back on the table with a heavy hand.

His father glared at him but said nothing. Alex led Elizabeth out of the dining room, but once they were out of his father's sight, he dropped her arm.

"You could have stayed with him if you wanted to," Elizabeth told him quietly, not wishing him to feel obliged to keep her company.

Alex looked as annoyed with her as he had with his father. "If I had wanted to I would have," he snapped. They went into the parlor, where he poured himself a large snifter of brandy, then threw himself into a chair near a window and proceeded to stare out into the darkness.

Elizabeth sat down on a settee near the center of the room, looking moodily about her. She remembered with longing the cozy evenings she and her mother had spent in Welford. The door opened, and she looked up as Alex's father entered. She gave him a smile of welcome that he ignored.

"You have a lovely home," she told him.

He glared at her and also poured himself some brandy.

"I am looking forward to seeing all of it," she continued brightly.

"I am honored," he said sarcastically.

Alex stared out the window, drinking his brandy, barely aware that Elizabeth soon excused herself and retired. He was concerned that his father's antagonism toward Elizabeth was so evident. How the hell was he going to be able to leave her here and go down to Brighton? Remembering suddenly that the house he had rented for Morgana would be standing empty since she was in mourning, he made a quick decision.

"You needn't worry that we shall intrude on your privacy much longer," he told his father as he rose unsteadily to his feet. "We merely stopped here on our way to Brighton. After all, it is customary that one's family welcome the new bride first . . ."

"I'm sure that Brighton will be delighted with her," His Grace said sarcastically. "No doubt she will become quite the talk of the town."

Alex pretended to accept it as a compliment. He bowed slightly to his father, then left the room.

After changing his clothes, Alex donned a dark blue velvet robe and poured himself a glass of claret from a crystal decanter in his room. He sat down near a window and drank thirstily, irritated that nothing was working out according to his original plan. Why should it worry him that Elizabeth and his father didn't get along? What the devil was he to do with her in Brighton?

He supposed that he had better warn Elizabeth that they were leaving in the morning, and, after downing the rest of the wine, he walked to the door that connected his room and hers.

After knocking sharply, he let himself into the room. Elizabeth's maid was just putting the last of her things away and with a knowing smile hurried out.

Elizabeth was sitting on the edge of her bed. Her hair had been carefully brushed and fell in long, soft curls over her shoulders and onto her breasts. Her nightgown was of a thin, white material with small rosebuds embroidered around the neckline. For some reason the flowers made Alex remember Elizabeth's mother, who had tearfully entrusted her daughter into his care. He felt a twinge of guilt at his treatment of her and frowned.

Thinking that he was frowning because of her, Elizabeth swallowed nervously. "Hello," she whispered.

Alex came further into the room, but with each step his purpose for coming grew dimmer and dimmer as his eyes took in the figure of his wife sitting on the edge of the bed, until he had completely forgotten about Brighton.

Elizabeth looked lovely, lovelier than he had imagined possible. Now that her hair was loosened from the tight knot she normally kept it in, it fell into thick curls that his hands longed to touch.

Elizabeth blushed under his steady regard and looked down at her hands, which were clutching the top of the coverlet nervously. There was only a single light in the room, a branch of candles flickering on a nearby table, which cast the room into deep shadow.

Alex took a few steps closer so that he was standing next to the bed. He watched the rise and fall of her breasts under the thin material and reached out a hand tentatively to touch her silken hair. She looked up at his touch, her eyes huge in her face.

Sitting down on the edge of the bed, Alex took one of her hands in his, pulling away the coverlet material that she was holding. "I won't bite you," he teased with surprising gentleness as his thumb softly rubbed the inside of her wrist.

She tried to smile. "I know. It's just that your father . . ."

"No," he said quickly, placing a finger over her lips. "We aren't going to think of him at all tonight." He bent forward and brushed her lips lightly with a teasing kiss while his right arm moved around her back to pull her closer to him until he could feel her soft breasts against his chest.

His lips became more insistent, moving sensuously against hers until they parted in response. Without even realizing it, he pushed her back into the pillows, so that his hands were free. He slid her nightgown off her shoulder, his hands delighting in the soft warmth of her skin. He kissed the little hollows along her neck.

When his hand slid under her nightgown, she started slightly. "No, no," he whispered. "Relax, darling. Just relax." His hands gently caressed her breasts, causing little shivers of excitement to race through her blood.

Elizabeth stared up at him in wonder at the feelings he was arousing. Her face was flushed and her eyes glowing. She had never experienced anything like this, never even imagined such feelings existed! Her whole body seemed to be on fire just from the touch of his hands!

As his lips bent down to hers once more, she timidly slid her hands under his loosened robe and felt the hard muscles of his shoulders with her fingertips. She was amazed at her own boldness, but her passion was like a heady wine that made her body seek pleasure while her mind's protests became fainter and fainter. She let her hands slide down his back to his slim waist.

Alex was vaguely surprised at her unrestrained response, but he was not inclined to give it much thought. There was something very potent in the feel of her slender body beneath him, and although his need to possess her was great, he also felt a strange tenderness toward her.

Gently his hands continued to explore her until he

had roused the sleeping passion in her and she responded eagerly to his caresses.

"Oh, Alex," she sighed, as he moved his weight more heavily on her. "I do . . ."

"Shush!" he whispered as his lips came down again on hers, kissing her deeply again and again, until she had no more breath to speak.

Later, Elizabeth lay with her head on Alex's chest, feeling deliciously drowsy. She remembered her initial distrust of him and smiled at how silly she had been, for he had certainly proven tonight just how much he loved her!

Feeling him stir slightly, Elizabeth turned her head to look at him. "Sometimes I can't believe all this," she said quietly.

"Hmmm?" Alex murmured, half-asleep.

"I mean, that you really love me," she explained. "Oh, I know that you said you did when you asked me to marry you, but I guess I was beginning to doubt it because you had been so cold lately. How was I to know that it was only because you were worrying about your father's reaction to our marriage?" she laughed softly. "But I know now that you really do, and I promise not to doubt you again." After sighing contentedly, she drifted off to sleep.

Alex lay perfectly still, staring up toward the ceiling in horror. Did she actually believe that he loved her just because he had made love to her? How could anyone be that incredibly naive?

When he was certain from her even breathing that she was asleep, he gingerly eased away from her. The unpleasant thought that perhaps her conclusion was not without some foundation flashed through his mind. After all, hadn't he made some rather wild declarations of his love before they married? And hadn't he meant her to believe them, not because they were true but so that his revenge would succeed?

He glanced over at her sleeping form and felt a sudden surge of desire, immediately followed by overwhelming guilt that the wine he had been consuming all evening did nothing to dispel. He was a bounder, a cad, he thought. He had taken an innocent young girl from her home and family, tricked her with his lies and taken advantage of her trusting nature to satisfy his physical desires! His father had called him despicable, but that was not strong enough to describe the level he had sunk to.

With a groan he swung his legs over the side of the bed and stood up. What kind of man had he become, he wondered, that he could so heartlessly use another person? After slipping on his robe, he hurried back into his own bedroom, wondering how he could ever face Elizabeth again.

CHAPTER SIX

Elizabeth stared at her reflection in the mirror, wondering with disinterest if the face looking back was really herself. There was a mild resemblance to the girl who used to live in Welford, but there also was a great deal that was different.

Her hair had been trimmed and styled, cut and curled, pinned and pulled until her scalp ached. Then the dressmaking had begun. She had had to stand for hours while every fabric and every color was tried, then selected or rejected—but not by her, of course. Her opinion was not sought once. Her wonderful, loving husband was ordering her remaking, she thought sarcastically.

Her husband! What a fool she had been, deluding herself into thinking that he cared for her just because he had made love to her! She had even stupidly decided that she was in love with him because of the feelings he had aroused in her. Luckily, though, she had never had the chance to tell him. There had been no need for words that night at Herriaton, and when she had longed to tell him the next day, the kind lover of the night before was gone and a cold, forbidding stranger stood in his place. Since then he had not come near her.

She glared angrily into the mirror, wishing she had never met Alex. He was everything she had suspected when they first met—cold, arrogant and selfish. She did not have the slightest idea why he had married her. He took no pleasure in her company, no pride in her appearance or accomplishments and apparently found her unsatisfying sexually, since he had shown no desire to return to her bed. Instead, he criticized everything that she did, and as soon as they had reached Brighton late last week, he had begun making her over. She could only assume that he agreed with his father about her shortcomings and was trying to change her into something passable.

"Oo, ya do look lovely," Elizabeth heard her maid cry.

Elizabeth opened her eyes in surprise. Her maid was standing back from her, looking on with approval. Standing up, Elizabeth took a quick glance in the mirror and smiled back at the girl.

"Yes, it looks very nice," she said and nodded. She supposed that the dark green dress she wore was becoming and that her new hairstyle was less severe, but it hardly seemed to matter.

Alex's arbitrary decisions about her clothing had been maddening for another reason, too. She had planned on using a good portion of her clothing allowance to replace the diamonds in the necklace, thinking that she would be given the money and left on her own to shop. Instead, the money never came near her. Dresses upon dresses were ordered for her, far more than she could ever wear, but she had no way to exchange some of them for diamonds. Replacing those paste stones seemed just as impossible as ever.

Elizabeth descended the stairs with a heavy heart. She was not looking forward to her first foray into society. Alex had told her that their hosts, the earl and countess of Hibbert, were warm and friendly people and that their parties were rarely dreadful squeezes, but such reassurance did not make her less apprehensive.

Alex was waiting for her at the bottom of the stairs. His eyes moved over her in cold appraisal, noting the way the satin clung to her high breasts and fell softly over her hips. Her thick brown hair was arranged in a simple, almost classical style that accentuated her slender figure and grace of movement. He frowned when he noticed the small gold locket she wore around her neck.

"Haven't you any jewelry?" he asked sharply.

Trying hard not to blush or become pale, Elizabeth shook her head. "Just this," she said.

"Blast!" Alex muttered. "I should have gotten some of the family jewels from Herriaton when we were there. There's some fool necklace that brides are supposed to get."

Elizabeth knew that she paled visibly, but she forced herself to smile as Alex helped drape her shawl around her shoulders and escorted her out to the carriage.

As they rode toward the party, Alex coughed hesitantly. "Are you nervous?" he asked suddenly.

"A little," Elizabeth said, staring out the window at the occasional lights they passed. "I won't know anyone there but you."

He coughed again. "Ah, yes."

She turned toward him. This uncertainty was not like him.

"You realize, don't you, that husbands and wives do not usually spend a great deal of time together at these affairs?" he said quickly. "Uh, some people might want to talk to me, while you will be making your own friends."

Elizabeth turned back to the window. "I see," she said simply. "You needn't worry. I shan't pester you."

"That wasn't what I meant," he snapped. "It's just that couples usually have their own friends. It's not as if I mean to run off the minute we are in the door. I will introduce you."

"How kind of you," Elizabeth drawled sarcastically.

Alex sat in silence, stunned by her sharp reply. Why was she so bitter? Wasn't his guilt and self-disgust punishment enough for his unspeakable behavior? A sudden thought jolted him. Could it be that she did not realize how sorry he was for the way he had tricked her? It was hard to believe that she could be so blind to his mental sufferings, but perhaps that was it.

He looked across the carriage at the dim outline of her figure. Maybe his way of showing contrition was all wrong. Perhaps instead of brooding he should be kinder, more gentle, more considerate. Then maybe someday she might be able to forgive him.

Pleased with his new plan, he made no mention of their little spat, and when they arrived he led her politely up to meet their hosts.

The earl and countess were a middle-aged couple dressed in varying shades of yellow, which matched the decorations in the ballroom.

"We are so happy to meet you," the countess cried as Alex introduced Elizabeth. "Everyone in town has been so anxious to meet you!"

"Why?" Elizabeth asked in astonishment.

The earl shook his head with a laugh. "All those women in there," he waved his hand toward the ballroom, "want to see what you have that they don't have."

Elizabeth still looked puzzled, but Alex tugged at her arm with a laugh. "I keep telling her what a prize she has won, but she doesn't believe me," he told the earl, conscious that Elizabeth was eyeing him in bewilderment.

As they walked into the ballroom, Elizabeth

turned to her husband. "Were you engaged to someone else before me?" she asked thoughtfully.

Alex stopped and stared at her. "Good Lord, no!" he said in surprise. "Why would you ask that?"

She shrugged her shoulders slightly. "I just thought from what Lord Hibbert said that someone else had hoped to marry you."

Alex took her arm again and glanced at the people in the ballroom. His lips twisted cynically as his eyes traveled over the crowd. "Any man who is older than sixteen, unmarried and with a respectable fortune has any number of women who hope to marry him," he noted harshly.

Elizabeth looked at him in surprise, understanding the current of bitterness in his voice. But as her eyes took in the beautiful women in the room, she wondered, too, why he had chosen her instead of one of them.

Much to Elizabeth's surprise, Alex stayed with her, walking around the room and introducing her to his friends and acquaintances. Some people seemed genuinely pleased to meet her, while others mouthed polite phrases as their eyes looked mocking. She did not understand all the undercurrents that she sensed and felt dreadfully out of place.

"Is turnabout to be fair play, then?" one outlandishly dressed man asked Alex as he kissed Elizabeth's hand.

Before Elizabeth could ask Alex what he meant, she was being pulled along to meet an elderly dowager who could not hear a word and had no idea who Elizabeth was.

A piano was hidden behind some potted palms in one corner, and a musician began to play a waltz. The earl and his wife danced for a few moments by themselves, then other couples gradually joined them on the floor.

"You can dance, can't you?" Alex asked her jokingly as he led her onto the floor.

"It's rather late to ask," Elizabeth smiled back at him, dazed by his attention. Was it all a pose for the people around them? "You know, the waltz was considered quite risqué back in Welford," she teased.

He put his arms around her, and they began to dance. She was a little uncertain at first, but he was a considerate partner. His hand on her back gently guided her steps.

Although neither of them spoke as they danced, Elizabeth was certain that he was enjoying her company. It was not just a pose or a pretense. He really was being patient and understanding with her.

As they completed their first circuit around the ballroom, she decided that all his former coldness had been caused by worry. He had feared that his friends might react to her as his father had. Now that he saw how well she was accepted, he would relax and enjoy being with her. By the time they were back on the far side of the ballroom across from the door, Elizabeth had forgotten the last few days of unhappiness. Then Alex stopped abruptly. He seemed to be staring over her shoulder at someone or something. She glanced behind her but saw nothing unusual.

"Is something wrong?" she asked, conscious that the other dancers were staring at them as they passed.

Alex looked back at her, startled by her voice. "Wrong? No, no, nothing's wrong," he said quickly. He suddenly realized that he still was holding her as if they were dancing and let go of her quickly. Then, taking her arm, he led her off the floor.

"Aren't we going to finish the dance?" she asked in bewilderment.

"Why?" He seemed surprised by her question. "I just wanted to be certain that you could show yourself creditably. I don't need to steer you around the floor for hours to do that."

His sudden reversion back to his former coldness so surprised her that she was speechless as he led her over to the deaf dowager.

As he unceremoniously dumped her on the settee next to the old lady, he bowed quickly. "Have a nice chat, my dear. I shall see you later." Then he turned and was lost in the crowd.

Alex reached Morgana before she had moved far from the doorway. She was dressed all in black, but few people would have called the low neckline and diaphanous material mourning clothes.

She was just turning away from an acquaintance when Alex came up beside her and took her arm.

"Morgana," he said in surprise, "I did not expect to see you here."

Morgana turned to look at him, her eyes cold and angry. "I don't see why not. We had this all planned," she snapped.

Alex frowned slightly, conscious of the people around them. "Let's go where we can talk," he said with a grim smile.

She shrugged but allowed him to lead her down a hallway and out onto the terrace.

"When I read of Francis's death, I had no idea that you'd come to Brighton," he told her as they sat on a bench in a deserted corner. "Although I am glad to see you. Brighton society is rather dull," he added.

"If you knew of his death, why did you stay away?" she cried angrily. "When you didn't come, I assumed you knew nothing of it."

"What did you expect me to do?" Alex asked her with a smile. "Come to the funeral?"

Clutching her hands in anger, Morgana stood up and walked a few feet away. "Yes, you could have. You knew that his family detested me. If you had any feeling at all for me, you would have wanted to be with me."

Alex could not help but laugh as he stood up also. "Having been your lover does not necessarily make me a pallbearer at your husband's funeral. I barely even knew him. I think my presence there would have been in questionable taste."

"Ah, yes," she said sarcastically. "You are always

the expert on what is proper and in good taste." She turned away for a moment, then, obviously regretting her outburst, moved closer to him. She kept her eyes down while her fingers played gently with the buttons on his waistcoat. "I missed you so, Alex darling," she whispered sensuously. "You must forgive me if I seemed a trifle short with you, but I've been so worried." Her fingers slid seductively across his chest.

He caught one of her hands and brought it up to his lips, kissing each of her fingers. "What was there to worry about?" he asked offhandedly as he turned her hand and kissed the inside of each wrist. "You knew what Francis's will said."

"Oh, not that." She dismissed her late husband with a shake of her head. "You had been so angry when I saw you last. I was afraid you were going to run out and do something foolish and ruin our splendid chance." She did not seem to notice that Alex had become quite still.

"Chance for what?" he asked ominously.

Morgana moved closer to him, the tips of her breasts lightly brushing his coat. "Now that Francis has died, there's nothing in our way. We can be together."

Alex dropped her hand and took a step away from her. "How long have you been in town?" he asked suddenly.

She peered at him through the darkness, confused by his abrupt change of subject. "I arrived today," she said impatiently. "I did go to the house you rented for me, but I saw a strange woman come out, so I went on to an inn. I have to admit I was angry at first," she admitted laughingly. "Surely you should have known that I would want to be here with you, but after I thought about it, I realized that perhaps it was for the best. It would cause a great deal of talk if I stayed in Brighton for the season. This way we can both leave quietly . . ."

"Morgana . . ." he interrupted her coldly.

"Perhaps we should go to one of your country homes. We can avoid a lot of gossip that way," she went on.

"Morgana," he repeated sharply. She stopped and looked up at him. "That woman you saw is my wife."

"Your wife!" she hissed, recoiling as if she had been struck. "How could she be your wife? It's only been a week or two since I saw you last. There's been no announcement in the papers."

"It's been three weeks," he corrected her impatiently, seeing no real need to explain the details to her. "You knew that I had to marry. As for the notice, I just thought to send it in a day or two ago, so it hasn't appeared in the paper yet."

"But Francis died right after you left," she argued. "If you had read about it, why didn't you come back?"

"What does Francis's death have to do with anything? My marriage does not affect our relationship at all." An idea suddenly came to him. "You didn't think I'd rush back and marry you, did you?" he asked her scornfully.

"I thought you cared about me." She made her voice sound hurt and bewildered. "You certainly led me to believe so."

Alex was neither an inexperienced greenhorn nor a bewitched old man. He was not easily manipulated or made to feel guilty, certainly not by someone as transparent as Morgana.

"I'm sorry if you feel cheated," he said forbiddingly. "I never mentioned marriage to you because, even if you had been free, I never desired to marry you. You had lovers before me. You knew exactly what you were getting into."

Morgana was livid with rage, but pride forbade her letting it show. She was silent for a long moment. Then she spoke, her voice soft and pleading. The slight tremor in it was supposed to be caused by embarrassment, not anger. "I certainly hope I haven't embarrassed you by my presumptions," she laughed. "I suppose Francis's death upset me more than I knew."

"Yes, that must be it," he said cynically. "I had better go back in." He picked up her hand and kissed it perfunctorily, then turned and went back to the house.

Once his back was to her, Morgana allowed her hatred to shine in her eyes. Her hands clenched into angry fists. "So I wouldn't have made you a good wife, would I?" she whispered harshly after him. "I can promise you that I'll be an excellent enemy!"

Elizabeth was surprised at the number of men who begged her to dance with them. She danced every set until her feet ached. Welford had never been like this!

But in spite of her astonishing popularity, she was not particularly enjoying herself. Her conversation was very stilted, for people were either asking her things that she considered private or making inane comments that she did not entirely understand. Finally, after smiling stupidly throughout a whole set at a man quite determined to embarrass her, she managed to slip away on the excuse that she wanted to tidy her hair. She ignored all his protestations of her loveliness and vanished into the crowd.

Once she was sure he was not following her, she began to look around her with interest. The house was spacious and richly furnished. Away from the ballroom were several smaller rooms, and she wandered along the hallway, glancing into them as she passed. One tiny one held a couple locked in each other's embrace. She hurried past, embarrassed by what she saw, but the couple had not noticed her momentary presence.

Another door led to a terrace lit only by candles inside paper lanterns. It looked pleasant out in the cool night air, but she was not so innocent as to believe that that was why most of the couples were out there. She hurried past that door, also.

She soon came to a larger room, where tables had been set up for card games. A number of people seemed to be enjoying them, for the room was crowded. Having seen all the gambling she had ever wanted to when her father was still alive, she was about to pass by this room also when she spotted her last dance partner coming down the hall toward her. He had not yet seen her, but he would in another moment. Although she chided herself that she was being cowardly, she knew that she did not have the experience to deal with such a determined flirt and darted into the game room.

Most of the people in the room were playing the games, but each table had a few people standing by, watching. Elizabeth joined the largest crowd, which had gathered around a man and a woman playing piquet. It was a game her father had taught her when he had been desperate for a partner, so she understood what she was watching. She had never played for any stakes, however, and thought five shillings a point seemed like deep play.

She watched the game with idle curiosity. She and her mother had suffered too much because of her father's gambling for her not to feel some disgust at the way these people carelessly tossed their money about. But she also found the game rather amusing. Neither player was very expert, and each made foolish discards that should have benefited his or her opponent, if that person had only been smart enough to see it.

The game ended a short time after Elizabeth began to watch. The gentleman totaled up the points.

"I fear you beat me rather soundly," he said with a laugh. "I owe you fifty pounds. Will you take my note?"

His partner laughed as she stood up. "How marvelous! Now I can buy that hat at Madame LeBeau's I fancied."

The two of them left the room chatting together, while those who had been watching either wandered over to other tables or went back to the ballroom—except Elizabeth, who was frozen where she had been standing.

Fifty pounds, she thought in total amazement. For just a few hours' play that woman had won fifty pounds! She said it was the cost of a new bonnet, but Elizabeth had a different measuring system. Fifty pounds was a third of the price she received for one of the small diamonds.

Was it possible that with a little luck and some skill (for surely she was a better player than those she had just watched), she could win enough money to replace the diamonds? She deplored gambling, but in this instance, mightn't it be permissible?

The idea was fascinating and growing more and more acceptable in her mind. If people wanted to throw their money away anyway, wasn't saving her mother and herself from prison a better reason for gambling than wanting a new bonnet?

She turned away from the table, eager now for the

opportunity to try her luck, and was startled to find someone standing next to her. It was a lady with vibrant red hair, dressed in a black dress.

"Good evening," the woman said with a warm smile. "Did I startle you? I didn't mean to."

Elizabeth smiled back, grateful for a friendly face amid all these strangers. "No, my mind was elsewhere."

The woman glanced down at the empty table with the deck of cards strewn across its surface. "Not on the cards, surely?" she laughed. "You don't look like a gamester."

"No, I was just watching a game," Elizabeth confided. "And—can you imagine?—someone won fifty pounds!"

From her tone it was evident that she regarded that a huge sum, but the woman just laughed. "Why, that's a mere pittance," she said. "Their stakes must have been awfully small."

"They were playing for five shillings a point."

The woman shook her head. "It's hard to find anyone willing to play for such low stakes now. Most people insist on ten or even twenty shillings a point."

"Ten or twenty?" Elizabeth whispered in astonishment. At those stakes that woman would have won a hundred or two hundred pounds. Why, she could buy back the diamonds even faster!

Unaware that she was being watched speculatively, Elizabeth could not control the look of excitement that crossed her face. Neither did she notice how the other woman's eyes narrowed or how her smile became less friendly.

"Perhaps I ought to introduce myself," the woman said. "My name is Morgana Tremayne. Lady Morgana Tremayne," she added with an embarrassed laugh.

Elizabeth smiled at her, liking her open friendliness. "I'm Elizabeth Waring," she said.

"Lady Elizabeth Waring," Morgana teased gently. "Yes, I have to admit I knew who you were. You have caused quite a stir, you know."

Elizabeth blushed with a sigh. "I really can't see why everyone is making such a fuss about me."

Morgana smiled but said nothing. She glanced down at the table again. "Were you hoping to find yourself a game here tonight?"

"Oh, no," Elizabeth cried quickly, suddenly uncertain. "It was interesting to watch, but . . ."

Morgana nodded. "The stakes are too flat. Yes, I certainly understand that. Who wants to win a hundred guineas when it could be five hundred?"

Elizabeth's eyes widened, and Morgana pressed on. "If you are interested in a friendly game, though, perhaps . . . No," she said quickly. "I'm sure you have other plans for tomorrow."

"Not that I know of," Elizabeth said quickly, curious as to what she was going to say.

"It's just that I was invited to a small card party. Just a friendly little gathering, you know. I thought you might enjoy it also," she said, watching Elizabeth closely.

"I don't know," Elizabeth hesitated.

"We will be playing for real stakes," Morgana pressed, not caring that that hardly sounded like a "friendly little gathering."

"No, it's just that I wasn't invited, and it seems rude to come without an invitation," Elizabeth explained.

Morgana laughed softly, but not in a way to offend. "No one will mind. We often bring friends along."

Still Elizabeth hesitated. She had a little money at her disposal that she could bring to begin play, but it was a drastic step for someone like herself, who disliked gambling. Then for some reason Alex's father came into her mind, and she remembered how rude and unwelcoming he had been to her. It would be just like him to punish her mother if he ever learned the truth. "I'll go," Elizabeth decided quickly.

"That's marvelous." Morgana's smile was radiant. "I will stop for you on my way there around nine." She was about to turn away when she stopped suddenly. "It might be best if you did not mention where you are going to your husband."

Elizabeth was surprised. "Why not?" she asked, worried lest she make some social blunder.

"Oh, it's nothing to be concerned about," Morgana laughed, reading her worried look. "It's just that he has the most phenomenal luck at cards, and we're all rather amateurs. If he knew about it, he might want to come, and then there'd be no chance for anyone else to win. And who wants to play if you can't win?"

Elizabeth still looked puzzled but nodded her head. "I shall keep it our secret," she promised.

"Good," Morgana said. "I will see you tomorrow, then." She smiled warmly at Elizabeth again, then walked slowly from the room.

Elizabeth watched her until she had disappeared around the corner, feeling much happier about the evening. Not only was she close to solving the problem of the diamonds, but she had found a friend, too.

CHAPTER SEVEN

Elizabeth was in high spirits when she came downstairs the next morning. By this time tomorrow all her worries about the diamonds would be over. Then she was going to prove to Alex and his father how wrong they both were about her.

Alex was drinking tea and paging through some correspondence when she entered the breakfast room. "I thought all you titled ladies slept till noon, and then sipped hot chocolate in bed," he teased with a smile. He seemed in an amiable mood.

Elizabeth smiled weakly at him, trying to cover her astonishment at his friendly teasing. "Perhaps I'm just not used to my leisurely life yet," she said, deciding to be equally pleasant. "By this time in Welford I was always up and about. There was so much to be done."

"Such as what?" he asked in surprise.

Elizabeth thanked a footman as he put a plate of eggs and bacon in front of her, then reached for a hot roll from the basket on the table. "Oh, about this time of the year, we'd be busy making jams and jellies and preserving the different fruits as they ripened. And there'd always be the cleaning and mending to do."

"But didn't you have servants for those things?" Alex asked with a frown.

Elizabeth stopped as she was spreading marmalade on her roll. "There was Bertha, of course. But she's getting older now, and it didn't seem fair to leave all the chores to her. Besides, what else was there to do?" She shrugged.

"There's not much jam making for you to do here in Brighton," he noted. "What will you do with your time?"

She took a bite of her roll and shook her head. "I don't know." She laughed after a moment. "Up until today I had fittings and appointments. I shall have to do some hard thinking."

"Since you have no plans, perhaps you would like to come for a drive with me this morning," he offered.

She stared at him blankly for a moment, dumbfounded by the invitation. "That sounds delightful," she suddenly rushed to accept.

He smiled back at her, then returned to his papers. Elizabeth began to eat again but watched him thoughtfully. He was in an especially pleasant mood this morning. Perhaps it would be a good time to talk to him—not about the diamonds, since she already had that problem solved—but about whatever had changed his feelings toward her.

"Alex," she said tentatively.

He put down the paper he had been reading and looked over at her. "Yes?" he asked when she was then silent.

Taking a deep breath, she plunged forward. "Alex, what's wrong?" She saw his puzzled frown and went on. "I mean, you're so distant at times, not like you were before we came to Brighton."

"And how was I then?" he asked. A sudden recurrence of guilt made his voice defensive and cold.

Elizabeth caught the hint of frost in his words but was determined not to let that stop her. "You were friendlier," she said, too embarrassed to point out that what she meant was that he had made love to her. "And you seemed to enjoy my company."

Alex's lips tightened slightly as he stared across the table at her. "And now?" His voice was deceptively quiet.

"You've been very generous," she said quickly, wishing that that cold look would go from his eyes. "But you seem so impatient sometimes. As if you were sorry that you married me."

Alex's eyebrows rose questioningly. "And did I ever say that?" he asked.

"No," Elizabeth said lamely. "But I was afraid you thought that from the way you acted."

Alex picked up his napkin and wiped his mouth carefully. He tossed it on the table before him and slowly stood up. "I fear your imagination is working too hard, my dear. I assure you that no such thought had ever crossed my mind." His voice was coldly forbidding rather than reassuring.

Elizabeth rose to her feet also. "I didn't mean to anger you," she said with a sigh and looked pleadingly at him. "I thought that maybe if we talked and I knew what was wrong . . ."

"Nothing is wrong, at least not that I know of," he snapped. "I am sorry if you find that your life is lacking in some way."

"No, no, that wasn't what I meant," Elizabeth cried impatiently. "In Welford you spent so much time with us, yet here I barely see you."

"It happens that I knew no one in Welford but you and your mother," he informed her. "Whereas here I have many social obligations. And I am afraid that I cannot abandon them all because you object."

Elizabeth clutched the back of her chair, trying to control her rising temper. "You are deliberately misunderstanding me," she accused. "I never suggested that you break off all your friendships. Surely you can have them and still be married."

"I would have thought so," he agreed coldly. "You were the one who was arguing the point."

"No, I wasn't arguing about your friends but about me," she tried to explain. "You act as if you are ashamed of me, as if you don't like me anymore. I'm not even allowed to choose my own clothes!"

Alex's smile was not comforting. "You had better

make up your mind, my dear. I can hardly be making all your decisions for you and neglecting you at the same time, now can I?" Without waiting for an answer, he walked quickly out the door.

Elizabeth stared in angry frustration at the closed door, sorry that she had ever brought up the matter. It had accomplished nothing but spoiling the amiable mood of that morning.

She threw herself back into her chair and angrily folded her arms across her chest. Alex was wrong. He *was* different since their marriage, except for that one night at Herriaton, and it didn't have anything to do with the amount of time he spent with her but with his attitude toward her.

Trying to talk about it was obviously not the answer. Well, if he was satisfied with their present relationship, then she would be, too. She was not going to beg for affection from him. He could ignore her from one week to the next and he'd not hear a complaint from her!

The whole idea of the marriage had been unbelievably stupid, Alex told himself as he restlessly paced his room. How could he have ever considered something so idiotic, let alone gone ahead and done it? What had started as an innocent joke had turned into a disaster, causing havoc in every part of his life.

Every time he moved, Elizabeth's presence as his wife was demanding something of him or requiring his attention.

Look at her clothes. What a mess she might have made of her new wardrobe if he hadn't seen to it. The same with her hair and the choosing of friends. She never said a word of complaint, he admitted bitterly to himself, but she was a master of lonely but brave expressions. She knew just how to make him feel like a churl, he decided, unwilling to admit that it was his own conscience that aroused the guilt feelings or that when he allowed himself, he did enjoy Elizabeth's company.

I've got to stop this, he said firmly, ceasing his restless walking. I've got to be firm and go back to my regular activities, pursue my interests and let Elizabeth occupy herself. Yes, that was it! He nodded. And the first thing he would do was visit Morgana.

After changing into a new deep red coat that admirably offset his silver waistcoat, Alex felt much more the thing. He had been too idle in the past few weeks, and that was why this whole business with Elizabeth was able to bother him. Once he had settled back into his usual routine, he doubted he would give her more than a passing thought each day.

Alex stopped in the hallway outside the library and pulled a pure white rosebud from a vase on a table there. He broke off the stem and fastened the flower to his lapel. Gazing at himself in the mirror, he was pleased with the results.

About to go down the final flight of stairs to the

door, he turned around when the library door opened and Elizabeth came out.

Her smile was determined. "Are you going out?" she asked politely.

Stiffening slightly, Alex prepared himself for an argument. "Yes," he said, glancing back in the mirror and making a minute adjustment to his cravat. "I'm going to visit a friend."

"That should be enjoyable." Apparently their ride had not been very important to him, she thought angrily, but she carefully kept all traces of her feeling from her face, looking down, instead, at the pen she carried in her hand. "I wanted to write to Mother but can't find a pen with a decent point. I think I have a better one in my room." She smiled as she went past him. "I hope you have a nice visit," she wished him warmly, then hurried up the stairs.

For a long moment Alex stared at her retreating back in disbelief, then turned and stomped furiously out of the house. Now what was he supposed to do, he fumed. How could he visit Morgana after Elizabeth had told him to have a good time? The very idea made his newly discovered conscience cringe. It ought to be a criminal offense to be so stupidly trusting as she was!

Instead of searching out Morgana, he walked quickly across town to Raggett's, where he happened upon Sir Matthew Denby. With his friend's help, he bet recklessly and drank heavily.

* * *

Elizabeth remained angry throughout the lonely afternoon. Her anger started to fade slightly as she ate her solitary dinner, and it was almost gone by the time she went up to her room to dress for the evening. She was sorely tempted to make some excuse to Morgana, for she was too depressed by Alex's hatred to go anywhere. It was only the thought of those horrid diamonds that made her decide to go through with the evening.

As she climbed the stairs to her room, Elizabeth found it was easy to build up her anger against Alex again. He certainly was not sitting at home worrying over their problems, so why should she?

Perversely, she chose to wear a pale green gown that she had bought against Alex's advice, and told her maid to arrange her hair in an intricate style she knew did not suit her. By the time Morgana came for her, she had successfully revived her anger against Alex.

"I'm so pleased that you're coming with me," Morgana said by way of greeting.

Elizabeth's smile was grimly determined, but Morgana did not notice.

"Is this party at the home of someone I met yesterday?" Elizabeth asked as they settled themselves in the carriage.

"No, I don't believe you have met Lady Eleanor Hardy yet," Morgana said, neglecting to add that "Naughty Nell" was not welcome in the same circles as Elizabeth.

"I do hope she won't mind a total stranger coming to her party then," Elizabeth worried.

"Goodness, no." Morgana laughed. "She just loves to meet new people. She simply adores it when her guests bring new people along."

Elizabeth thought it seemed very strange, remembering the problems that unexpected guests would cause her and her mother. But then people were very different here in Brighton, as she was learning.

Since Brighton was not very large, it took them only a few minutes to reach Lady Hardy's establishment. There were a number of people walking up to the door, which was standing open, while a burly footman stood next to it. Amid a great deal of shouting and laughter, Morgana and Elizabeth were helped to alight.

A gentleman walked by them and up the steps to the house. So close that she was nearly in his pocket was a young lady of either questionable fashion sense or questionable morals. Her gaudy red dress must have been made for her when she was at least a stone lighter, for with her every movement, she threatened to burst out of it. Although the young lady appeared to be unaware of the danger, all the men present noticed and watched with avid interest.

Shocked by such goings-on, Elizabeth hung back, her determination wavering. Surely this was not the type of party she ought to be attending.

Morgana had been prepared for such last-minute uncertainty and smiled reassuringly at her. "Oh, pay no mind to them." Elizabeth still looked uncertain. "Alex finds them so amusing," she added slyly.

Elizabeth did not think it strange that Lady Tremayne called Alex by his given name. "Alex has been here?" she asked suspiciously.

"Oh, yes," Morgana nodded. "He comes here quite often."

Elizabeth eyed the young girl again with an unfriendly glare. So Alex frequented places such as these, did he? Yet he could not be bothered even to take her for the ride he had promised!

"I don't think we ought to stand about here on the street," Elizabeth told Morgana purposefully, moving toward the door. The burly footman did not stop them, and they proceeded up the inside stairs to a large hallway, off which opened many smaller parlors.

Glancing into one of the rooms, Elizabeth saw several tables of people playing cards. They were not quiet and restrained as she had expected but shouting loudly to others across the room and drinking freely of the wine that seemed to be everywhere.

Hearing people speaking of E.O., faro and roulette, Elizabeth felt twinges of vague uncertainty about being there, but Lady Tremayne looked quite at ease. Well, Elizabeth thought, if Alex was too busy to advise, she would just have to rely on someone who did not think she was a bother, and that was Lady Tremayne.

"May aye take yer thengs?" a young maid asked

of the two women. "Er do ya want me ta show ya ta the ladies' room?"

"No, you may take them," Morgana said quickly, wanting to get Elizabeth into the gaming rooms and seen as soon as possible. What scandal was there if she hid the whole evening? "We want to go right in and play." Morgana gave the maid her shawl and waited while Elizabeth did the same.

"This is ridiculous!" Alex laughed rather disgustedly as he and Denby left Raggett's. "I have never won this much money before. Even when I was playing carefully."

"Well, you weren't playing carefully today," Denby noted. "Your mind seemed to be miles away, while mine was right where it should have been, for all the good it did me. Perhaps I should marry, too, and then have an argument with my wife. Maybe that would improve my game, also."

Alex stopped walking and turned to his friend. "I never said I had argued with Elizabeth," he said, slightly irritated.

"Didn't need to," Denby said with a laugh. "It's written all over you. You're worried that she's still angry with you. Why don't you just go home and beg her forgiveness? I've no doubt you were in the wrong, anyway."

"Oh, for goodness' sake," Alex said in exasperation. He walked angrily across the street, but Denby followed him.

"Take some of that money you won and buy her something she can't resist," he suggested. "You've certainly had enough experience wooing reluctant women. You ought to be able to win over your wife. After all, this time you can do your persuading in private."

"I don't wish to discuss my marriage with you," Alex told him coldly. "It is merely one of convenience, yet you seem determined to make it into something else."

"Don't get all hoighty-toighty," Denby laughed. "I know you, remember, and I know that you could have married anytime in the last three years. All you had to do was crook your little finger at a woman and she would have raced to the altar with you. Why, suddenly, after seeing all those women, would you marry someone you barely knew?"

"If you remember things so well, you might think back to the evening we were at St. Martin's Place . . ."

Denby shook his head. "Oh, that nonsense. Of course, I remember it, but I don't believe a word of it. And I doubt you really do. No, there's only one reason you'd marry any girl and that's because you wanted to."

Alex snorted rudely. "You must be foxed!"

"Face it, Alex," Denby grinned. "If you had only wanted to anger your father, you could have found dozens of simple ways to do so. You married your cousin because you wanted to and only because you wanted to."

Alex glared at him, then began to walk more briskly. "Doesn't Nell Hardy have some sort of gaming house around here?"

Denby nodded, and they turned down the next street and walked for a few minutes. It was not hard to find the house they sought. It was the only house on the block that was well lit, and several carriages pulled up while they were approaching.

"It looks like the rooms should be bursting tonight," Alex noted with enthusiasm. "I shouldn't have any trouble finding some game to my taste."

"If all you want to do is throw your money away, I'd be glad to relieve you of it right here," Denby offered.

Alex never could stay angry with Denby for long. "I don't think that would quite satisfy my restlessness," he said with a laugh.

"And gambling will?" But Alex was not listening any longer.

Although neither of them was known personally to the footman at the door, the man did not stop them. It was obvious from their expensive clothing and air of assurance that they had money to play with.

Once they were in the house, Alex looked around him. A number of people had arrived just before them and were being greeted by Lady Hardy. She looked vaguely familiar to Alex, and he had a slight recollection that she had been involved in some scandal in London a few years ago. He turned away, not particularly interested in his hostess, and caught a faint whirring noise.

"Is it possible that they have a roulette wheel here?" he marveled to Denby.

But his friend was not listening to him. "Alex!" he whispered harshly and grabbed his arm. "My God, Alex, look!" He was staring across the room.

Alex followed the direction of his eyes and found himself staring at Morgana. "Damn!" he muttered. "Why does she have to be here? I'm getting a little tired of seeing her every place I go!"

Denby stared at him as if he had lost his mind. "Not her, you nodcock! Look who's standing next to her!"

Morgana moved slightly as she handed her shawl to the waiting maid, and Alex could now see who was next to her.

"My God!" he gasped, paling as he caught sight of Elizabeth. "What the hell is she doing here?"

With Denby following close behind, Alex rushed over to where the two women stood, grabbing Elizabeth's shawl out of the startled maid's hands.

"I hope I haven't kept you waiting long, my dear," he said pleasantly as he tossed the shawl around her shoulders.

Elizabeth just stared at him in surprise as he firmly took hold of her arm.

Morgana flashed him a look of complete hatred

but smoothed out her features almost at once. "Why, Alex," she purred, "have you come to join us?"

"No, that pleasure is mine, Lady Tremayne," Denby said smoothly, taking her hand and putting it on his arm. He appeared not to notice her angry scowl. "I had so hoped that you would favor me with a game of piquet."

"How lucky for you, Lady Tremayne, for I fear we must be leaving," Alex said smoothly.

Before Morgana could argue, Denby was easing her away from Elizabeth, whom Alex was hurrying down the stairs. Luckily he had not recognized anyone else waiting in the hallway. But as he hurried her down the outside stairs, two men were alighting from a carriage, and they both knew him well.

"Blast!" he muttered, and practically shoved Elizabeth down the remaining steps. "Wait over here and be quiet!" he ordered as he pushed her quickly into the shadows alongside the house. The two men casually walked up the stairs and entered the house.

Once they had gone inside, Alex breathed a sigh of relief. Pulling her away from the house, he kept a firm grip on her arm and led her briskly down the street.

When no one was near them, he turned to her impatiently. "What the hell were you doing there?" he snapped, carefully keeping his voice low.

His effort to remove her from the scene without attracting attention had not been lost on Elizabeth, but she had spent all afternoon wishing he still loved her, and his rage only made her see how foolish she had been. "What do you suppose I was doing there?" she hissed back. "I was invited."

"Invited!" he cried. His father's words suddenly came rushing back. "And you just couldn't wait to start throwing my money away!"

Elizabeth glared at him the best she could in the darkness. "I brought my own money to bet," she informed him. "I wasn't using any of yours."

Glancing about quickly for carriages, Alex pulled her across the street. "Of course not," he sneered. "And you weren't going to lose anyway, right? Is that why you and your mother lived in such appalling conditions? Because you had gambled away her income?"

Elizabeth was so shocked that she could not speak. She stammered incoherently, longing desperately for something heavy to hit him with.

"After all your mother must have suffered because of your father's gambling, you have to subject her to more!" The disgust was quite plain in Alex's voice.

"I am not a gambler!" Elizabeth cried out, twisting her arm furiously, trying to free it from his grasp.

"Waring! Is that you?" A male voice called out from a few houses down the street.

"Blast!" Alex swore again, and pushed Elizabeth into the shadows of a doorway as the man approached.

"Are you going over to 'Naughty Nell's'?" he asked.

Alex forced himself to laugh. "No, I've spent the day at Raggett's," he said.

The man laughed also. "And now you're to pieces," he finished for him. Obviously having seen something of Alex's companion, he glanced toward the shadows where Elizabeth was. "And you've got more interesting things planned, eh, Waring?" He laughed rudely. "I couldn't believe it when I heard you had married, but I should have known you'd never let it interfere with your life," he snickered loudly, then with a wave wandered across the street toward the gaming house.

"Why didn't you tell him I was your wife?" Elizabeth whispered angrily as she came out of the shadows.

Alex was watching his friend's progression across the street. When he was safely out of earshot, he turned impatiently back to her. "Having an argument with my wife outside in the street in this neighborhood would attract much more attention than being seen with a strumpet!"

"I see," she said stiffly. "There's nothing unusual in that, is there?"

Alex snorted in irritation and grabbed her arm again. "I am not going to stand here arguing with you. It's become quite damp out. I would much prefer to be in bed right now. My own bed," he snapped quickly before she had a chance to speak.

Elizabeth's feet were wet and cold from all the puddles and muck that he had dragged her through, but she was still so angry that she barely noticed it. "If you are so tired, I should have thought you'd have been on your way home, not going to a card party."

"Oh, yes, you'd have liked that, wouldn't you?" he fumed. "You could have squandered half my fortune and created a scandal serious enough to ruin your reputation in society. And I thought when I married you that you had some sense," he added.

The inference that she had no sense made her angrier than the accusation that she would have lost so much money. "I have plenty of sense, I'll have you know. And I also had some doubts about the propriety of such an establishment. What I did not have," her words were ground out slowly and distinctly, "was someone to ask about it. Since I failed to take advantage of the brief audience I was granted with my husband this morning, I had to rely on the advice of a friend."

"And just who is this marvelous friend who advised you to ruin your reputation?" he asked.

Hearing it put like that, Elizabeth had a moment's hesitation. "Lady Tremayne," she told him, a hint of uncertainty in her voice.

"Morgana!" he cried incredulously. "She's this wonderful friend you're entrusting your reputation to?"

They turned a corner, and a stronger wind bore down on them. It chilled Elizabeth to the bone; her feet were numb with cold. Although she was still angry with Alex for his neglect of her, she could see how foolishly she had behaved. She stumbled slightly on some garbage that had been thrown into the street.

Alex stopped walking and glanced at her. She did not know if he was aware of her shivering or had just decided that they had come far enough from the gaming house. He flagged down the next hackney that came by and roughly bundled her up into it.

"Morgana," he said again, as if he could not believe that Elizabeth would have trusted her. "Didn't you think it strange when she invited you to a party at someone else's house?" he asked her in the darkness of the carriage.

Elizabeth sighed wearily. "She was very friendly," she said lamely.

"And you didn't wonder why?" he cried.

The cold, her wet feet and Alex's strange behavior were suddenly too much for her. She hated Brighton and wished she had never met Alex. Slow, silent tears began to run down her cheeks. Although it was too dark for Alex to see her, she turned her face away from him. "Yes, that was certainly stupid of me, wasn't it?" she whispered, trying hard to keep her voice steady. "In a town full of strangers, one person seems friendly to me, and I conclude that she is sincere." Her effort was spoiled by her loud sniff.

"Oh, damn!" Alex muttered, and tossed his handkerchief into her lap. A wife was far more trouble than he had ever imagined.

CHAPTER EIGHT

Alex rose early the next morning. He had slept little and thought far too much. It was a relief to get up and try to find some occupation to stifle his thoughts.

There was no reason Elizabeth should still be on his mind. Good Lord, he had slept with a number of women before and none of them had preyed on his mind so! Why, even when he was asleep, she crept into his thoughts! He was having the most alarmingly vivid dreams of making love to her, and the frightening part was that he did not know if he was remembering things from that night at Herriaton or was dreaming them as he wished they had been. And he did not feel at all guilty when he awoke.

He also should not be feeling responsible for last night's fiasco. It was hardly his fault that she was incredibly untutored in the ways of society. She had seemed so sensible since their marriage, it was hard to believe she could have acted so stupidly last night.

Morgana's behavior should not have come as any surprise to him, though. She was no innocent to the ways of society, and her sudden befriending of Elizabeth was nothing more than an attempt to hurt him. He knew now that she had hoped to marry him, and it was not like her to suffer her disappointments with silent bravery.

The more he thought about Morgana, the less attractive she seemed to him. How had he ever become involved with someone so unfeeling? Look at the way she had treated her husband, and the unscrupulous way she was going to use Elizabeth because she was angry at him. Why, the woman had no feelings at all. The sooner he broke off with her, the better they would all be. In fact, he would do it this morning. He would buy her some sort of gift, a bracelet, perhaps, and get her out of their lives completely.

The thought that she still might cause some mischief worried him, though. How the devil was he to keep watch over Elizabeth all the time? What she needed was some older woman to teach her all the things her mother should have.

Of course, Alex thought suddenly. That might be the best solution. He would bring her mother down here. There was plenty of room in the house, and they could go about together, which would free his time. Her mother could teach her the things about society that had never come up in Welford.

Pleased with his plan, Alex ate a quick breakfast, then left the house. First he would break off with Morgana so that his position with her was very clear.

Walking briskly across town, Alex went to a jeweler he occasionally frequented when he was in Brighton. He quickly chose a gaudy, wide gold band studded with diamonds and some other jewels. That should ease any emotional pain that Morgana might be suffering.

As he was waiting for the bracelet to be wrapped, a long string of pearls with matching earrings caught his eye. He had not intended to buy Elizabeth a gift, but rose-tinted pearls such as these were unusual, and they would look lovely with a deep red velvet evening dress that Elizabeth had ordered. Besides, as Denby had reminded him, it was partly her fault that he had won so much last night. He would spend some of it on her.

To his disappointment, the clasp of the pearl necklace was loose, so he left it to be repaired, promising to call for it when he returned to town. He took the earrings and Morgana's bracelet and left the shop.

Early in the morning was not the best time to call uninvited upon a lady, but that fact would not have stopped Alex if he had but known where Morgana was staying. He tried several of the more elite inns and a few of the not so posh ones, but there was no trace of her. He could hardly go from door to door asking for information of her. He wanted to end their affair discreetly, not publicly announce that they had had one. Finally he was forced to admit defeat and return home.

After telling his valet to pack a bag for him, Alex wandered down to the breakfast room for another cup of tea. He hoped Elizabeth would be up before he left—but only because he wanted to warn her to stay away from Morgana, he quickly assured himself.

Elizabeth was not only up but in the breakfast room already. When he entered, she jumped nervously to her feet. She was pale and had shadows under her eyes, as if she had not slept well. He frowned when he that saw her plate of food had been pushed away untouched.

"Aren't you eating?" he asked.

Ignoring his question, she plunged into a speech that sounded as if it had been rehearsed. "I'm terribly sorry about last night," she said in a rush. "I never dreamed it was not a proper place to go, but I realize now that it was a horribly stupid thing to do. If you never forgave me, I would understand," she added bravely.

Alex's lips twitched slightly at her seriousness, conveniently forgetting his own anger. "Why don't we just forget about it?" he suggested.

She looked at him hesitantly. "Then you aren't angry any longer?"

He shook his head. "I was not really ever angry at you," he said.

"You weren't?" she asked, clearly skeptical.

A footman brought Alex a cup of tea, and he waited until the man had left the room again. "Well, perhaps a trifle disappointed, but I did know it was not truly your fault."

Elizabeth still looked disbelieving, but she allowed the subject to drop, pulling her plate over to her again and beginning to eat.

"I'm afraid I shall have to leave town for a few days," Alex told her as he stirred his tea.

She put her fork down slowly. "Is it because of last night?" she asked.

He looked surprised. "No, no," he said, shaking his head, then realized that wasn't strictly true. "It's a problem at one of my estates," he improvised quickly.

She looked immensely relieved. "I really thought I was such a bother that you needed a rest from me," she confided. "But I guess it would be far easier to just banish me than to leave yourself."

"I doubt I'd ever go as far as banishment," he said with a laugh.

She ate in silence for a few moments. "I shan't go anywhere while you are gone," she said suddenly. "Then I will be certain not to get into another fix."

"You needn't go to that extreme," Alex said and laughed again. "I was merely going to suggest that you check over your plans with Mr. Clifford. He has been with me for years now and can safely guide you while I'm away." The thought that she might be offended by having to report her doings to his secretary suddenly occurred to him. "If you wouldn't mind, that is," he added uncertainly.

"Oh, no," she said quickly. "I think it's a good idea, although I can hardly rush back and check out each new acquaintance with him. Perhaps he could write up a list of respectable people for me, or a list of unrespectable ones, if that would be shorter. Each time I was introduced to someone, I could check to see if that person has your approval."

Alex burst into laughter. "Think of the scandal if your list was misplaced and people realized that they did not have my approval! Or there might be a great rush to curry my favor, so that they would be on the good list."

They both were laughing together when a light knock was heard at the door. Alex's valet stepped inside. "Sir Matthew Denby is here, m'lord, and your horse is ready," he said.

Alex nodded and quickly finished his tea. He stood up and looked across at Elizabeth. "I had better see what Denby wants, and then I shall be off," he said.

She rose to her feet, also, and stood watching him. He was conscious of a reluctance to leave her and walked slowly around the table until he was at her side. Her eyes followed him as he moved.

He leaned forward and slowly let his lips touch hers in a gentle kiss. It was over quickly, but he could still feel the softness of her mouth on his.

Elizabeth's eyes were wide with some emotion he did not understand, but when he leaned forward again, her body swayed toward him. He caught her in his arms and held her close, letting his lips find hers once more.

This kiss was rougher than the first and demanded

a response from her. But it made him feel vulnerable, too, as if he was not totally in control of the situation. It gave her some power over him.

Drawing back slowly, Alex stared into her flushed face and sparkling eyes. He had a lively desire to forget about his trip and stay here with his wife.

But realizing that this trip was necessary for her sake, he took a step backward, bumping into a chair. It scraped along the floor with a loud screech. He glanced about, startled.

He tried to think of something witty or sophisticated to say. "I . . . uh . . . should be back soon," he mumbled.

Elizabeth nodded, seeming unable to say anything.

Remembering suddenly about the earrings he had for her, he reached into his coat pocket. "I've something for you," he said quickly, and he held out the package.

She took it silently and unwrapped the small box. The two earrings lay inside it. "Oh, they are beautiful!" she whispered, turning them about slowly.

She glanced quickly around the room, hurried over to the mirror that hung behind the buffet and put them on. Turning her head from one side to another, she admired her new jewelry with a pleased smile. "Oh, they look so lovely," she purred.

The pearls seemed to take on an added glow from the warmth of her skin. Alex smiled at her enthusiasm, not wanting to diminish her excitement by telling her of the necklace.

"Be good while I'm gone," he teased as she walked back to her place at the table. He leaned forward and kissed her cheek quickly.

"Good-bye," she said. Her voice reflected her disappointment at his going. He smiled back at her and let himself out of the room.

Elizabeth sat down in her chair in a daze, her fingertips lightly touching her lips. She could still feel the tingle of his kisses. Was it possible that he was beginning to care for her, she wondered. If only he weren't leaving, she might be able to make him want her as he had that other night! She blushed at her bold thoughts. Oh, how she wished she were going with him!

Well, why not, she thought suddenly, sitting up a little taller. They could spend a little time together away from the pressures of society or his father. Perhaps in the right circumstances, he might drop the cold, remote attitude completely, and they could enjoy each other's company.

Jumping up from her chair, Elizabeth ran soundlessly across the floor and into the hallway. She hoped he hadn't left yet.

She could hear voices coming from the library down the hall, and she hurried along toward it. As her hand touched the knob, the door moved slightly, for it had not been closed all the way. The voices became clearer.

"I think I shall forever remember Brighton as the town of mix-ups," she heard Alex say with a laugh.

Elizabeth smiled to herself. She was feeling rather confused these days herself. Her hand went to the knob again.

"How was I to know that she would still want this house?" Alex went on. "I know that I promised to rent it for her for the summer, but after Francis died . . ."

Elizabeth's hand slid from the knob, although her body stayed frozen by the door.

"Quite so," Denby agreed.

"Then last night I could hardly run up to her and demand to know where she was staying in town. Considering the way she had publicized our relationship, that is something I should have known," Alex said.

"Not to mention her companion," his friend added.

"Oh, yes, that would have led to some questions I am certain I can live without," Alex returned.

Elizabeth frowned. Whom was he talking about? And what kind of relationship did they have? She heard someone moving about the room, and then Alex spoke again, but his voice was too low to hear all that he said.

". . . not that it has anything to do with my marriage," he ended more loudly than he had begun. "But we need to have a talk. I don't want another fiasco like last night. Lord, I nearly stopped breathing when I saw her standing next to Elizabeth!"

Who was next to me last night? She tried to remember.

"My mistress and my wife—together! What a fright!" Alex laughed.

Elizabeth became deathly pale and could not have moved to save her life. His mistress! Horrors! It must have been Morgana! No wonder he thought it so funny that she called Morgana her friend and did not want her to associate with Lady Tremayne. Think how embarrassing that could become for him!

She realized that Alex was speaking again. "This should ease any pain she might be suffering," he said; then she heard the faint rustling of paper.

"My, my," Denby said softly. "Diamonds, rubies and emeralds. That should ease a great deal of pain."

"Yes, she's quite easy to please," Alex said, but Elizabeth missed the sarcasm in his voice, for she was too conscious of the pain she was feeling.

Footsteps started to come near the door, and she backed away slowly, almost numbly. "So while I'm gone, see if you can find out where she's living. I shall be in your debt forever."

"And will I get a bracelet like that one?" Denby said, and he laughed.

Elizabeth suddenly realized they were coming out of the library and would find her there unless she hid. She looked around frantically, knowing that she could not face anyone, especially Alex, after what she had heard. She was trembling violently and felt absolutely wretched.

The nearest room was too far away. That left the stairs or a window just next to her. Knowing that if she went down the stairs, Alex would be following in a moment, she darted over to the window and pulled out the full satin drapery. Just as she threw herself behind it, she heard the library door open, and two sets of footsteps entered the hall.

She held her breath nervously, blinking away the tears that kept forming, as the two men stood for a moment at the top of the stairs. She did not know what she would say if she were discovered.

Finally she heard the men walk down the stairs, and she breathed a sigh of relief. Slipping out from the drapery, she was about to rush up to her room when the open library door beckoned.

She moved slowly across the hallway, listening for anyone coming her way, but the only sounds she heard came from downstairs, where Alex was preparing to leave. She tiptoed into the room.

It was empty, as she had assumed it would be. Although she was made nervous by the thought that someone might find her here, she did not seem able to leave but kept walking slowly forward toward the desk.

She stopped when she came right up to it. The top was empty except for a few writing tools and a small stack of books. The bracelet was not there.

"How stupid!" she whispered to herself. "What did you expect? That it would be left out here for you to see?"

Walking slowly around the desk, she pulled back the chair and opened the top drawer. It contained nothing but writing paper. Feeling only slightly guilty about searching Alex's desk, she pulled open the second drawer. A small box lay inside.

Elizabeth stared at it for a long moment. Did she have any right to look at Alex's gift for someone else? But, then, did he have the right to give such gifts to other women? She reached for the package and placed it on top of the desk.

It took her only a moment to unwrap the bracelet. It was a wide band with countless jewels fashioned to represent flowers. Rubies formed the petals, diamonds were the centers and emeralds made the leaves of the plants.

Elizabeth stared at it. She knew little about jewels, the Herriad Necklace being the only other piece she had ever looked at closely. She thought this piece was too gaudy, but there were so many stones in it that she thought it must have been very expensive. Alex must care a great deal about Morgana to buy her such an expensive piece.

Forgetting her earlier desire to keep her presence a secret, Elizabeth wandered across the room to a window and stared out aimlessly.

Why had Alex married her if he was in love with someone else, she wondered. Alex had acted as if he cared about her when they were in Welford, and that one night . . . But since they had come to Brighton, it was not hard to believe that he was thinking of someone else. She rubbed her forehead thoughtfully. Hadn't they mentioned someone dying? Could they have been in love and her husband have died just after she and Alex had been married? But that would not explain why he had married her in the first place.

She leaned her forehead against the cool glass of the window and let the tears fall that had been threatening. Why had she been such a fool as to forget all her suspicions of him and let herself be swayed by his occasional amiable moments? Instead of using the common sense that she had prided herself on, she had acted like a romantic idiot, allowing herself to succumb to his charm. She had even found all sorts of excuses for his strange behavior, but had never suspected the truth—that he was regretting his marriage to her now that his mistress was free.

Just because she had had to marry him because of the diamonds did not mean that she had to make a complete fool of herself. She should have guarded herself against his flattery and been glad that he spent so little time with her. Then she could have laughed secretly when it appeared that he was sorry they had married, and his love for Morgana would not have bothered her at all.

Standing up, Elizabeth took a deep breath. Tears would not help her. She caught a gleam of light that was reflected in the window and put her hand up to her ear questioningly. She felt the pearl earring. Very slowly she pulled one off, then the other, and stared down at them in her hand.

Suddenly all the hurt and agony faded as fury took their place. He bought an expensive bracelet for his mistress, and two tiny pearl earrings for his wife! That was how much he valued her!

Admitting to herself that she knew nothing about the relative values of pearls, diamonds and rubies, she judged by the look of each piece. She put the earrings down next to the bracelet and stared at them. Anyone who chose the pearls over the diamonds would be a fool. Why, the bracelet had—she counted quickly—it had thirty-six rubies in it, eighteen emeralds and six diamonds. While the earrings— She stopped and picked up the bracelet again. Carefully she counted the diamonds. Yes, there really were six.

Almost as if the bracelet had burned her skin, she dropped it on the desk and backed away from it. No, she couldn't do it, she told herself. It would be wrong. Even if Alex did have a mistress, she should not interfere.

But, then, she argued, where should her loyalty lie? With Morgana, who had tried to disgrace her? With Alex, whose loyalty to her prompted him to buy her a pair of pearl earrings when he squandered half his fortune on a gift for his mistress? Or with her mother, who was the one person who really did care about her?

The answer was obvious. Elizabeth scooped up the bracelet and raced up the stairs to her room. The Herriad Necklace was about to lose its six paste stones and get some lovely new diamonds in their place. Morgana and Alex would get exactly what they deserved—some cheap imitations!

CHAPTER NINE

Morgana tapped her foot impatiently as her eyes wandered over the crowded Assembly Rooms.

"If you are looking for Waring, you won't find him," a voice said at her side.

Morgana's lips tightened in irritation, but by the time she looked up at the well-dressed gentleman next to her, she was smiling pleasantly. "Why, Sir Quentin," she welcomed him. "It has been such a long time since I've seen you."

Sir Quentin Paine sat down on the chair next to her. "Waring's gone," he repeated, watching her face for any sign of surprise. He saw none.

"Now, surely you don't think I was unaware of that fact," she teased lightly.

"He's married now," he grumbled.

"I know that, too," she said smoothly, turning back to watch the crowd, although with Alex gone there was little point.

"There was a rumor that you didn't know until it was long done," he remarked.

Morgana turned to him, her eyes flashing angrily. "I knew of his intention to marry long before his bride did," she snapped.

Sir Quentin waited for her temper to subside before speaking again. "Why don't you come with me?" he said softly. "I'd treat you better than he ever could. There's talk he's going to drop you, anyway."

Morgana's anger was under control, but just barely. "Oh, there is, is there? And does he think he can just drop me whenever he chooses? Have I nothing to say on the matter?"

"Has he ever given much heed to your wishes?" Sir Quentin asked slyly.

Morgana stared into the crowd, remembering how amused Alex had appeared at her small shows of independence, but he had had a will of iron in other, more important matters.

Correctly reading her silence, Sir Quentin went on. "Everything must be done his way. He thinks he's the only one with any sense or judgment. I saw how he tried to keep your relationship hidden away."

Morgana glared up at him, but he knew her anger was directed more toward Waring than himself. "Perhaps you should find someone else, someone who could please you more than he could. What a blow to his pride." He laughed quietly.

Watching him speculatively, Morgana smiled slowly. "Perhaps," she shrugged. "And I suppose you would be that better man?"

He nodded as she turned back to the crowd. "I

don't think I'm quite finished with him yet," she murmured, then caught sight of a graceful figure on the dance floor. "Just look at her," she hissed disgustedly to her companion. "That is what he prefers!"

Sir Quentin watched Elizabeth dance with interest. Her dark blue dress was highlighted with silver embroidery around the neckline and hem, and her dark hair was arranged in a simple coronet on the back of her head. She moved with a unique grace and elegance that gave her a beauty far different from most of the women present. He could see why Waring had chosen the delicate-looking lady that he married, but he wisely did not admit this to Morgana. He might admire Elizabeth, but it was Morgana's lusty charms that he desired.

"Maybe you want to make him just a little sorry that he didn't choose you?" Sir Quentin suggested quietly.

Morgana did not reply immediately but instead looked at her companion thoughtfully. He was an attractive man, wealthy and quite generous. He could be a useful ally. She decided to confide in him.

"I already tried that," she admitted carelessly. "But Alex was too quick for me."

"He's not here now," he reminded her softly.

"How true!" Morgana agreed with a smile that faded suddenly. "But he's sure to have warned her. She would not be so trusting this time."

"Ah, but you have me now," he noted. He turned

to find Elizabeth among the dancers on the floor. "Am I right in supposing that the little lady's name is to be disgraced?"

Morgana made a great show of playing with her fan. "It's not that I want it to happen," she protested innocently. "But Alex did seem to feel that she was much more suited to be his wife than I was."

Sir Quentin laughed. "And that stung, did it?"

She frowned at him. "If you are only going to laugh . . ."

"No, no," he said and shook his head. "You see before you a man of purpose. All I need from you is your promise."

Morgana looked puzzled. "My promise?"

"That you'll reward me handsomely for my services."

She smiled shyly, looking over the top of her fan at him. "Why, how could I resist someone so masterful?" she purred.

Elizabeth returned to her seat next to Lady Torrington. She and her husband, Lord Torrington, were old friends of Alex and his father and had insisted on having Elizabeth for dinner and taking her to the Assembly Rooms while Alex was gone.

The Torringtons were in their fifties and devoted to one another. Both were gentle and thoughtful, reminding Elizabeth of her mother. (How they ever became friends with people like Alex and his father she would never understand, for they were so different.) Sincerely delighted to meet her, they were obviously pleased with Alex's choice of a wife. After all the opposition that she had encountered, it was wonderful to be accepted—although, after learning the truth about Morgana, it was hard to smile and agree when her hosts sang Alex's praises.

"It's a pity Alex is not here," Lady Torrington said with a sigh as Elizabeth was returned after a dance. "He is much more handsome than that last fellow."

Elizabeth smiled briefly and turned away. Luckily she did not have to answer, for another man came up to beg a dance with her. He was the baron of something or other; she could not quite remember his full name. Lady Torrington laughed as Elizabeth stood up to dance.

"If Alex doesn't come soon, you'll forget what he looks like," she said.

If only I could, Elizabeth thought as she was led out to the dance floor. After the dance the baron offered Elizabeth a glass of punch, which she gratefully accepted. As he led her toward the refreshment table, he told her about his estate. She was listening with only half an ear when she saw another man approach them.

"I say, Colburn," he said, giving Elizabeth the baron's name finally, "you must introduce me to your lovely companion."

The baron turned to find a very large man before them, smiling hopefully at Elizabeth.

"Lady Waring," the baron said, "this is Sir Quentin Paine." His voice was not particularly welcoming, but Sir Quentin paid no attention.

"Might I beg the honor of a dance?" he asked.

Elizabeth nodded, for the baron had become a trifle tedious with all his talk of horses, and this man had such a friendly smile. She allowed him to lead her onto the floor for a country dance.

The steps of the dance did not keep them together very much, but Elizabeth knew that Sir Quentin watched her the whole time. Not that there was anything wrong with that, for he seemed eager only to please. He greatly reminded her of a big friendly dog that one of the farmers in Welford had had.

It was almost at the end of the dance that the accident occurred. Sir Quentin was dancing with her when he accidently collided with another couple. He was horribly embarrassed, for he had caused a scene, but he felt even worse because he had trod on her foot.

"I'm fine," Elizabeth said with a laugh. "It's a little sore, but nothing more."

"I might have hurt you terribly," he cried. "I shall never forgive myself for my clumsiness. Let me find a place where you can rest."

"That's not necessary," she assured him. His concern was most touching. "I shall just go back to Lady Torrington."

"No," he cried, holding her arm.

She looked at him, puzzled.

"You will be pestered to dance by all sorts of foolish young men, and you'll get no rest," he explained. "At least sit for a few minutes before going back there."

Elizabeth could not resist such pleading. "It is not necessary, but it would be pleasant to be away from the crowd for a few minutes."

He smiled down at her and led her out a conveniently near doorway. There were a number of people walking down the hallway, going to and from the ballroom. He quickly led her down another, quieter hallway and into an empty sitting room.

"It is very quiet here," Elizabeth said as she walked stiffly over to the settee in the middle of the room. Her foot was beginning to ache, and it was a relief to sit down.

"I knew it was what you really wanted," Sir Quentin said as he sat down near her.

Elizabeth gave him a puzzled look, which he returned quite innocently.

"The furnishings are quite lovely," she said, gazing about the room. "Not what I would expect in public assembly rooms."

He suddenly moved closer. "Not nearly as lovely as you, my dear."

Elizabeth's eyes widened in shock as she faced him. "Sir Quentin!" she cried. She tried to move away from him but found that he was sitting on the edge of her dress. "If you please, sir, I should like to go back to the others!"

"Not yet, my lovely, not yet," he whispered thickly. Moving closer and closer to her, he pressed her back into the corner of the settee, his large hands holding her down.

"Let me go," she hissed at him, squirming to try to get free. He was much too strong for her, though, and he laughed at her feeble attempts.

His lips landed on hers, and she turned her head from his repulsive touch. While he rained kisses on her neck and along her cheek, she pushed against his chest with all her strength, but it seemed to make no difference to him.

"So you're not the cool statue that you seem, are you?" he said, lifting his head slightly and looking down at her. She shivered at the look in his eyes, which only seemed to amuse him. "I should have known that Waring would choose someone with fire."

While his right hand held her back, his other hand twisted tightly into her hair to hold her head still.

Elizabeth's anger turned to terror. She tried to twist herself free and heard her dress rip. "Please let me go," she pleaded.

His lips came down on hers again, and this time she could not move because of his hand in her hair. His tongue pushed against her mouth, trying to force it open. Oh, Alex, she thought frantically, if only you would come like you did the last time when I was in trouble. But Alex was far away, and she was alone in Brighton.

As Sir Quentin shifted his weight slightly, a sudden memory came back to her. It was something she had seen her father do once to disarm a man. It had proved amazingly effective. Grasping at the chance she was given, she brought her knee up very sharply and very accurately. Sir Quentin slid away from her, doubled up in pain.

"Why, you bitch!" he muttered.

She tried desperately to pull her dress out from underneath him. Just as she freed it, his hand darted out and grabbed her arm.

"So that's how you play, is it?" he snarled at her.

Suddenly the ornate top of a gentleman's walking stick was placed firmly against Sir Quentin's chest, and a male voice stopped him. "I think you had best remove your hand from this lady," someone said. Although it was cool and calm, the voice held authority, and Sir Quentin obeyed.

Elizabeth backed out of Sir Quentin's reach before she turned to see who her rescuer was. It was Alex's father.

"Good God!" she whispered as she stared at him.

His lips twitched slightly. "Not quite, my dear." His smile faded as he took in the fear in her eyes and her pale face. "There is a mirror on the far wall," he told her.

She walked hesitantly over to it and glanced at the sight of her mussed hair and swollen lips. Her hands were trembling slightly, but she forced herself to smooth her hair back into place as best she could.

The tear in the shoulder of her dress was small, and she pulled the edges together, hoping it would not show. Then she turned back to His Grace.

She was surprised when he held out his arm for her to take. She hurried over to it, grateful for his support, even if she was not sure why he was offering it.

"Why, is something wrong in here?" a familiar voice said from the doorway.

Elizabeth turned to see Morgana and an elderly woman just inside the room.

"Lady Waring, are you all right?" the older woman asked. "Lady Tremayne said you were ill and asked me to come sit with you."

Elizabeth felt His Grace stiffen. "I fear someone must have misunderstood, Lady Agatha," he said with a polite smile. "It was not my daughter who was ill but this young man." He nodded to Sir Quentin, who was still standing near the sofa. "I do hope you are feeling better?" he inquired with apparent concern. "And I certainly hope your illness does not return," he added meaningfully.

Sir Quentin glared at him and shrugged his coat back into place. "If you ladies will excuse me?" he said and, bowing, he swiftly left the room.

Lady Agatha watched him leave, then turned back to Elizabeth. "If you are certain that you are all right . . . You do look a little pale," she added.

"No, I am fine," Elizabeth insisted. She had the most curious desire to burst into tears, but she managed to smile at the old lady.

But Lady Tremayne was not so easily fooled. "I had no idea you were in town," she said to His Grace.

"I am hurt," he mocked her. "I thought my comings and goings were of such importance to you."

"How fortunate that you both were here when Sir Quentin became ill. I'm not sure that Lady Waring could have coped alone," she sneered.

"But how wrong you are!" the duke said smoothly. "Elizabeth is remarkably resourceful. It's one of the reasons Alex loves her so much."

Elizabeth blushed at so blatant a lie, but Morgana did not challenge him. She gave him a frozen stare, then hurried from the room, followed by Lady Agatha.

As soon as they had left the room, Elizabeth's composure failed her. She began to tremble again, and she clung to His Grace's arm.

"Where the devil is my fool son?" he snapped at her, his sympathetic manner gone.

She took a deep breath and looked up at him. "At one of his estates," she gulped. "He left two days ago."

"One of his estates?" he asked. "How can that be when I just received a message from his agent?"

Elizabeth stared at him for a moment, then shrugged her shoulders. "Well, at least he isn't off somewhere with Lady Tremayne," she said, then burst into tears.

"Come, come, now," His Grace said sharply.

"This will never do. We can't stay in this room forever." That had little effect on her tears. "For goodness' sake, girl, if you insist on making a spectacle of yourself, I shall leave you here alone!"

Elizabeth forced herself to stop, although she looked quite bedraggled. "I'm sorry," she whispered, and she wiped her face with the back of her hand.

"That does not help," he said impatiently, and, taking out an immaculate white handkerchief, he wiped her cheeks. He was surprisingly gentle, and tears formed again in her eyes.

"If you start to cry again, I shall hit you," he snapped.

Elizabeth smiled wetly at him. "I don't believe you."

He chose to ignore her remark and put his handkerchief away. "Now we are going to walk out of here, and you are going to act as if you are dressed to meet the king," he said briskly. "There will be no crying and no cringing. If anyone speaks to us, we will stop to chat, and you will smile and laugh. Do you understand?"

"Yes," she whispered, nodding her head.

He squeezed her hand and led her to the door. Pasting a bright smile on her face that she thought must look ridiculous, Elizabeth walked proudly through the Assembly Rooms. His Grace kept them walking, but not so quickly as to attract notice. No one stopped to speak to them, so Elizabeth's smile was not challenged.

Their carriage seemed a haven of safety, and Elizabeth sank back into the cushions with a sigh of relief, while His Grace sent a message to the Torringtons.

"Now, why the devil did you go into that room with that man?" His Grace snapped as the carriage door was shut.

"He stepped on my foot," Elizabeth said wearily.

"He what?"

"He stepped on my foot while we were dancing, and he wanted me to sit down and rest," she explained.

"And you believed that?" he asked in astonishment.

Of course she had believed it, she thought angrily. Why else would she have gone in with him? "In Welford a gentleman would not maul a lady, especially after he had stepped on her foot," she informed him.

"This is not Welford," he noted dryly.

"Oh, I know, I know." Her voice lost its anger. "But I wish it were. How I wish I were back home where I belong!"

If His Grace was surprised by her sentiments, he did not express it but sat in silence as the carriage clattered over the streets.

"What brought you here to Brighton?" Elizabeth asked suddenly. Now that she was safely away, her spirits were returning.

"I read that Sir Francis Tremayne had died."

"Morgana's husband? Not you, too," she added in disgust.

"No, most assuredly not me, too," he agreed quickly. "Lady Tremayne and I have an active dislike of each other. I came because I feared she might cause trouble between you and Alex."

"And so you rushed down to stop her?" Elizabeth's voice was clearly skeptical. "From what you said at Herriaton, I should think you would be delighted if our marriage was a disaster."

"Let's just say that I have come to regret my harsh words and realize that Alex may, indeed, have chosen wisely."

Elizabeth was not fooled by his smooth tone. "He might have married Morgana, you mean," she said. "And that would have been worse than me."

The carriage pulled to an abrupt halt before the rented house. "Here you are," His Grace said as he climbed down. He turned to aid her.

"Aren't you staying here also?" she asked. The porter opened the door to the house, and light streamed out onto the steps.

"Here?" His Grace looked surprised. "No, of course not. I took a room at an inn."

"But why?" she asked. "We have enough room here."

"Perhaps I would prefer an inn," he told her curtly.

She took a deep breath and tried to ignore his rudeness. "At least come in for a few minutes," she invited him. "I do believe Alex has some brandy that you could sample."

He agreed and followed her into the house. The butler took his hat, gloves and the walking stick he carried. Then Elizabeth led him up the stairs to a small parlor.

"The brandy is there, if you would like some," she offered, pointing to a table in the corner as she sat down. "I never did thank you for your help tonight," she said quickly, her eyes on her hands clenched tightly in her lap. "I don't know what I would have done had you not been there." She frowned as a glass suddenly came into her sight. "What is this?" she asked, looking up at him.

"A brandy," he said. "I think you need it more than I do."

She looked at it uncertainly, then took a small sip. "It's awful," she gasped.

"Drink it anyway," he ordered.

Another small sip was all Elizabeth could manage before she put the glass down on the table next to her.

"You remind me of your mother," he said quietly as he watched her.

Elizabeth's eyebrows rose in astonishment. "I don't look anything like her!" she pointed out.

"I never said you did," he noted.

"And I don't act anything like her!" she continued. When he said nothing, she looked away. "Just how do you think Morgana is going to cause trouble?"

"She may do nothing." He shrugged, putting his glass down.

"You did not come all this way to Brighton because you honestly believed she would do nothing!" Elizabeth scoffed. "What kind of trouble could she cause? After all, Alex and I are married. There is nothing she can do to change that."

His Grace came over and sat down across from her. Her simplistic views irritated him. "She can use her influence over Alex to keep him away from both you and me. She might even induce him to fly to the Continent with her."

Elizabeth stood up impatiently. "You make it sound as if Alex has no say in the matter. I doubt that he would allow her to lead him along like some little puppy!"

"He is extremely devoted to her," he noted.

Elizabeth walked around her chair to face him from behind it. "Then why didn't he marry her?"

"Perhaps he did not know of her husband's death until it was too late," he said bluntly.

Elizabeth's face became pale, and she sat down slowly. That was one possibility she had never even considered. "You certainly are a great comfort to me," she said ironically.

"I think it is most likely, however, that most of her anger is directed at you, for you took the place that she wanted. Or perhaps she wants to punish Alex for not marrying her."

"That sounds like a strange way to love someone," Elizabeth noted.

"Love?" His Grace scoffed. "Who's talking about love? Morgana never loved anybody in her life, except herself. You can be certain she's not suffering from a broken heart because Alex married you. It's only hurt pride." He walked across the room, poured himself some brandy, then came back to sit down before her.

"Well, whatever her feelings, I don't like her. If she really were a nice person, she would not have pretended to befriend me as she did."

His Grace's eyebrows raised. "And when was this?"

Elizabeth blushed a little, for she had forgotten that he knew nothing of the incident. "It was a few days ago," she said quickly. "She invited me to go to a party with her. I was going to ask Alex if I should, but we argued and . . . Well, I just went. It turned out that it was not the sort of place I should have gone. Luckily, Alex was there and took me right home before anyone could notice."

"And just what kind of place was this?"

Elizabeth looked him straight in the eye, refusing to flinch from his anger. "It was a gaming establishment."

"A gaming den!" he cried. "And then that episode tonight! The devil! You don't need Morgana to disgrace you—you're bound to do it yourself!"

Elizabeth rose slowly to her feet, anger blazing

166

through her. "I can only be blamed for my inexperience!" she told him coldly. "It is true that my reputation was in jeopardy, but only because I believed what people said to me. I didn't realize that I had to mistrust anyone who seemed slightly friendly." She took a deep breath to ease away some of her anger. "But now that you are here, I need not worry about that any longer."

His Grace jumped to his feet also. "What the devil are you talking about now?"

Elizabeth's smile did not reassure him. "It's quite simple," she said calmly. "I have no idea where Alex is or when he will return. He advised me to check my activities with his secretary, but you saw tonight that pitfalls can still arise. Now that you are in Brighton, I have an exceptional escort for parties and an excellent guide as to whom is socially acceptable."

"You expect me to escort you about?" he cried in astonishment.

Refusing to appear ruffled, Elizabeth nodded quietly as she sat down and folded her hands in her lap. "Yes, I think you could foil any further trouble Morgana tries to make."

"But I have no desire to take you about," he announced, flinging courtesy aside in favor of truthfulness. "I have disliked your domineering ways from the first time I set eyes on you. I am not about to welcome your companionship."

"Oh, you might dislike me," Elizabeth noted with a flash of anger in her eye, "but I think you would dislike a major scandal even more. If Morgana should succeed the next time she tries to disgrace me, I won't be the only one hurt. It will reflect on you and Alex as well."

He was silent for a moment, staring down at the floor. Then he lifted his head and looked directly at her with a frown. "What makes you so certain that I will agree to this outlandish scheme? I could just go back to Herriaton."

"Because you care about Alex," she said simply. "And no matter how much you dislike me, I think you know that I would not do anything deliberately to hurt him."

She looked directly at him, waiting for some sort of reply. He finally nodded grudgingly. "No, I don't suppose you would."

"So you must help me avoid the places where I might accidentally hurt him. And maybe, if we work together and do not fight, we can win him away from Morgana."

He frowned at her for a long time, and Elizabeth began to worry. Was he going to refuse?

"What did your mother tell you about me?" he asked suddenly.

Elizabeth stared at him. "About you?" She shook her head, trying to remember her mother mentioning him at all. "Nothing that I can remember," she said.

"Nothing?"

Her mother's conversations about the necklace she had stolen were not what she would choose to retell, and she squirmed uneasily. Surely her mother must have said something repeatable at some time.

He mistook her silence for her mother's silence. "And your father? Did he ever speak of me?" he sighed.

"Oh, yes," Elizabeth nodded quickly. "About how your grandfather left you all his money instead of dividing it. It was his favorite topic."

His Grace played with his glass on the table before him, avoiding her glance. "And did you think it was unjust, also?"

"I didn't see that it mattered." His Grace's eyes flew up to hers, and he saw a flicker of humor there. "There would have been nothing left by the time I was born, anyway."

A reluctant smile played at the corner of his lips. "Tell me, did you bully your father the way you intend to bully me?" he teased, beginning to feel a grudging respect for her.

The humor left Elizabeth's face. "It is impossible to appeal to someone's better nature if he has none," she stated. "Does this mean you will help me fight Morgana?"

He shrugged. "Just what do you expect me to do?" he asked in resignation.

"You will move in here with us tomorrow," she announced calmly, "and show everyone what a happy family we are."

"And how will you convince Alex to join this masquerade?" he asked.

"I shan't have to," she replied with a smile. "When he sees that you have actually accepted me as his wife, he will have no more reason to quarrel with you."

"You make it sound remarkably simple," he said skeptically. Picking up his glass, he quickly drank the rest of his brandy. "Why are you doing all this?" he asked. "You could sit back and wait until he tired of her himself, or just ignore the whole situation, like most women do."

"I am not a very patient person," she said. "And I have never been able to sit back and wait for things to happen. There's too much risk of having fate decide against you."

"I was wrong," he said quietly. "You aren't anything like your mother," he said as he put his empty glass down.

Her laugh was one of real merriment. "I do believe I mentioned that."

A smile twisted his lips as he bowed and left the room. He wondered if Alex had any idea what his wife was really like.

CHAPTER TEN

As Elizabeth was eating her breakfast the next morning, His Grace's luggage arrived along with a curt note saying that he had some business to attend to and would see her later in the day. She smiled as she folded the piece of paper and picked up her cup of tea. It was strange that she should find herself depending so heavily on the one person she had detested for years. She only hoped she was not wrong in trusting him.

While she was personally supervising the cleaning of His Grace's room, Elizabeth was surprised to hear a carriage stop before the house about an hour later. She had not expected him so soon.

Taking a quick glance in the mirror to repin a few errant curls, she hurried into the hallway and down the stairs. She stopped halfway down in total surprise, for it was not His Grace who was being shown into the house but her mother!

"Mother!" she cried happily, and she ran down the rest of the stairs.

Margaret looked up as her daughter hurried toward her and dropped the hatbox she was carrying. "Libby!" she called, just as she was enveloped in an enthusiastic embrace.

"Oh, Mother, this is a wonderful surprise," Elizabeth said, stepping back slightly. "Did you just decide to come visit us? Oh, but Alex isn't here," she added in disappointment. Suddenly realizing that she was blocking the doorway and that a footman was waiting to carry in one of Margaret's trunks, she moved aside quickly, holding onto her mother's hand. "I do hope you're going to stay for a while so you'll be here when he returns."

"Libby," her mother said quietly, "Alex brought me here."

Elizabeth's face registered her total surprise. "Alex brought you?" she repeated dumbly. "You mean he went to Welford and asked you to come?"

"Of course. I wouldn't have come without being invited."

"But . . ." Elizabeth looked up and saw Alex standing in the doorway, watching them. Her hold on her mother's hand tightened slightly. "Good morning," she said uncertainly, remembering all that had happened since he had gone.

Alex smiled and walked into the foyer. "You look so serious," he teased. "And your mother's arrival was meant to be a pleasant surprise."

"Oh, it is," she quickly assured him with a smiling

glance at her mother. "I just don't know what to say."

"How about 'welcome home'?" he teased, and leaning forward, he kissed her cheek.

She blushed. "Welcome home," she whispered.

Looking at the trunks and boxes piled about the foyer, he shook his head. "I do hope we have a room large enough to fit all this," he grinned.

"Oh, a room!" Elizabeth cried, her hand covering her mouth. Both Alex and her mother turned to stare at her. His Grace was due to arrive any time now! How was she going to explain his presence to Alex and her mother?

"Take my mother's bags up to the room across from mine," she instructed the butler quickly. "And tell the maids to air the bed."

"Isn't that room rather small?" Alex asked with a frown. "Surely she would be more comfortable in the other bedroom."

Finding it impossible to explain that she had already given his father that room, Elizabeth searched frantically for some other excuse. "But she'd be so far away from me," she said weakly, as if the further ten feet would tax her mother's strength. Turning to her mother, she asked, "Would you like to use my room to freshen up?"

Margaret nodded gratefully. "That would be nice."

Elizabeth took her quickly upstairs, conscious that Alex was looking at her strangely. At least once they were in her room, she would have a chance to warn her mother of His Grace's impending arrival.

Her mother had other plans, though, and as Elizabeth closed the door behind her, Margaret turned around and faced her angrily.

"Libby, how could you?" she scolded fiercely. "How could you take those diamonds and sell them?"

Elizabeth just stared in dismay at her mother for a long time. There was little sense in pretending to misunderstand, for her mother looked determined to learn the truth. Sighing, she walked wearily across the room and sank down onto the edge of the bed. "Who told you about them?" she asked.

"Ben did," Margaret said impatiently. "And you needn't get angry at him. He was worried and only did what he felt was right."

"And I only did what I thought was right," she said stubbornly.

Margaret came over and sat down next to her. "But Libby, they weren't even ours."

"How was I to know that?" Elizabeth cried defensively. When Margaret blushed, she softened her tone. "Father left us nothing. Nothing but debts. There was no other way for us to have money to live."

Margaret shook her head. "There's always another way," she pointed out gently. "Have you told Alex?"

"There was no need," Elizabeth shrugged. "No

one ever asked for the necklace, and anyway now the diamonds have been replaced."

"With Alex's money?" Margaret asked suspiciously.

Elizabeth stood up and walked restlessly away from her mother. She was aware of a slight twinge of guilt about replacing the stones from Morgana's bracelet, but she tossed her head defiantly. If Alex had not been buying jewels for his mistress, she would not have been able to do it. "Why not with his money? He's not the saint you seem to believe he is. His behavior has not been perfect."

"He's very devoted to you," Margaret scolded.

Elizabeth looked skeptical.

"He is," her mother insisted. "Why do you think he came to get me? He's very worried because you are so ill prepared to take your place in society."

"Perhaps he's afraid some mistake of mine might reflect poorly on him," Elizabeth grumbled.

"Libby, that's not fair. Why are you so determined to think the worst of him?"

"Why are you so determined to sing his praises?" Elizabeth returned irritably.

Margaret stared at Elizabeth's sullen face from across the room. Suddenly she began to laugh. "My poor Libby," she said, shaking her head. "You've always made the decisions, haven't you? How hard it must be for you to find that your happiness lies in someone else's hands and that there's nothing you can do about it!"

Elizabeth turned away and began to fuss with some combs on her dresser. "I don't know what you are talking about," she said.

But her mother was unimpressed. "Oh, yes, you do. I saw the way you looked at Alex when he came in. It is quite obvious that you love him. Actually, I was relieved to see it," she said with a laugh. "Ever since Ben told me about the diamonds, I was afraid you had married Alex because of them. I could have cried for happiness when I saw the love on your face."

"Really, mother." Elizabeth was exasperated. "I would have thought that living with Father would have cured you of these romantic fantasies." She smoothed some imaginary wrinkles in her skirt. "I had better tell the cook that we've two more for lunch. Come down whenever you're ready," she added.

Margaret smiled, not the least bit perturbed by her daughter's forbidding attitude. "I am glad to be here," she smiled at her. "I've missed you."

Elizabeth turned at the door. "I missed you, too," she said, then slipped out.

"I couldn't believe it when Alex told me that you had been invited to a reception at the Pavilion," Margaret sighed as they ate lunch. "My daughter—a guest of the Regent!"

Elizabeth smiled weakly. How was she going to tell them that Alex's father was coming soon?

"But you must come with us," Alex insisted. He looked over at Elizabeth expectantly.

"Oh, yes," she hurried to agree. "I would love to have someone there with me whom I know."

Alex frowned, and she knew that she had said the wrong thing. "I did not invite her so that I could be free," he said reprovingly.

Elizabeth bit her lip nervously. "No, that wasn't what I meant," she hurried to explain. Voices suddenly came from the hallway, and, hearing his father's voice, she looked at Alex fearfully.

He, too, recognized the voice. "What the devil . . . ?" he said, standing up.

The door opened, and a footman entered. "His Grace has arrived, m'lady," the footman said, as Alex's father pushed past him and into the room.

"Told the fool I didn't need to be announced." He stopped short as he suddenly saw his son standing at the head of the table.

Alex looked likely to order his father thrown out of the house, so Elizabeth jumped to her feet. Running over to His Grace's side, she threw her arms around him. Her actions successfully astonished everyone into inaction.

"Why, how wonderful to see you!" she cried, and she kissed his cheek. Slipping her arm through his, she looked up at him with every evidence of affection. "I did not have time to tell them the surprise yet."

"What surprise?" Alex asked coldly, eyeing his

father with active dislike and his wife with astonishment.

Covering his initial surprise well, His Grace smiled fondly at Elizabeth before turning to his son. "Elizabeth has invited me to stay here with you while I am in Brighton."

Alex looked dumbfounded, but Elizabeth ignored him and turned to her mother, who was gazing in horror at His Grace as if he were some sort of demon about to devour them all. Elizabeth gave her an encouraging smile. "Of course, you remember my mother," she said.

To her surprise, she felt His Grace stiffen as he noticed her mother sitting quietly across the room from them. "Good day, Margaret," he said quietly. "You are looking well."

Margaret was ghostly white as she glanced up at him, then back down at her plate. "Good day," she gasped, her fingers nervously playing with her wedding ring.

His Grace suddenly seemed to withdraw. "I had not realized that you already had a guest," he said. "I'm sure that with your mother here, you would prefer me to go back to the inn."

"Of course not," Elizabeth cried, before Alex could agree and send him off. "We have more than enough room."

"Perhaps I should go to an inn. I wasn't going to stay more than a day or so, anyway," Margaret blurted out nervously.

Elizabeth scowled at her mother. "Don't be silly. You brought enough luggage for a year, and you both are staying with us." She turned to one of the footmen serving lunch. "Please set another place for His Grace."

Glaring mutinously at both Alex and her mother, she led His Grace to the place across from her mother, while the footman set out silverware and dishes for him.

"Isn't this going to be fun, all of us here together?" she enthused as she sat down again. Alex looked far from pleased, while her mother stared blankly down at her plate. Elizabeth looked purposefully at His Grace, hoping he was not going to be as difficult as the others.

"Have you any plans for this afternoon?" she asked cheerfully as she began to eat the piece of cold meat pie on her plate. "Perhaps we could all do something together."

No one's face lit up at the idea, but His Grace did grunt some sort of agreement.

"Maybe we could go on a drive around the city," she suggested. "I've been here for several weeks already, but I haven't seen much except the insides of ballrooms. And I'm sure mother would like to see the sights, also."

"I could arrange for a carriage," His Grace grudgingly offered.

Alex took a long drink of ale. "I have already made plans for this afternoon."

His Grace's eyes flashed with annoyance, but Elizabeth allowed him no chance to speak. Giving him a quelling glance, she turned to Alex. "That's perfectly all right," she said, and she smiled understandingly. "After being out of the city for the past few days, we know you must have more important things to do than go sightseeing with us."

Her willingness to exclude him made Alex frown slightly. He did have to see Morgana and that could not be postponed, but it would be nice to think that his presence would be missed, even slightly.

Margaret looked up from her plate. "I don't think I will go, either," she said timidly.

Elizabeth turned to her, hiding her impatience. "Don't tell me you have already made plans, also," she teased.

"Perhaps we should just not go," His Grace snapped. "If no one wants to . . ."

"No, we are going," Elizabeth interrupted curtly. She turned back to her mother, her manner much more gentle. "Now, why didn't you want to go?" she asked.

Margaret looked about, nervously aware that everyone was watching her. "It's just that I'm rather tired. After the trip and all . . ." Her voice died away uncertainly.

"Why, that's no problem," Elizabeth laughed. "We'll let you rest for a while after lunch and go out later in the afternoon. Will that suit you, Your Grace?" she asked.

"Whatever you wish," he grunted. He looked over at Alex as he had a sudden thought. "Perhaps by that time you will be free."

"Oh, I doubt it." Elizabeth shook her head quickly. "We mustn't pester Alex so. He has more important things to do than be bothered with our little outings," she laughed.

By now Alex was definitely annoyed. He had been ready to agree, although grudgingly, to accompanying them if they went in the late afternoon. Several hours spent in his father's company was not a pleasure he greatly desired, but it appeared that no one wanted him along, anyway. "It's so kind of you all to be so understanding about my other commitments," he said sarcastically.

"We know how busy you are." Elizabeth smiled sweetly down the length of the table at him.

"I trust I can finish my lunch before my busy schedule calls me," he noted.

"Oh, certainly." Elizabeth's smile was innocently puzzled.

"Oh, come now, Morgana. I'm certain you can spare a few minutes to talk with me," Alex snapped impatiently. He was standing in a not-too-private hallway of the inn where she was staying, while a curious maid openly listened to their conversation.

A coach pulled up outside noisily, and its passengers began to wander into the inn. A portly gentleman dressed in black and yellow eyed Morgana with interest. She flashed an inviting smile at him, casually redraping her shawl around her shoulders, then turned back to Alex.

Sensing his irritation, she smiled slightly. "But I had no idea you were coming, and I made other plans. As you can see, I'm on my way out." She sighed regretfully. She would make him pay for his neglect of her of late. He needn't think he could ignore her and then, whenever he chose, pick up their relationship where it had left off. No, she would decide when to favor him again.

"Then change them," he demanded. He looked around him. Spotting Morgana's portly admirer, he glared fiercely at him until the man hurried away. An elderly couple had also entered the inn and were standing a little way back, watching him. He turned back to Morgana. "Isn't there someplace we can talk? Someplace private?"

She shrugged unconcernedly. "I suppose we might go up to my room," she suggested, watching him slyly. He did not appear to be as delighted with the idea as he should have been.

"No, not there. Doesn't this damn inn have any private parlors?"

The elderly woman at the door was either shocked at his language or Morgana's suggestion. She hurried her husband away, muttering quietly to herself.

"This is it." Morgana was losing patience herself. "I am sorry if my lodgings do not please you, but since the house I had rented was given to someone else, I did not have much choice."

He took a deep breath and tried a different approach. "I have something for you," he said quietly, patting the pocket of his coat. "And this is hardly the place I had hoped to give it to you."

The idea of a present brightened Morgana's eyes. "The only place that we can be alone is my room," she said with a smile. "Unless we prefer to wait until a private parlor is free, and that could be hours." She glided over to him and took his arm. "Shall we go up?"

"No," he said, pulling away from her slightly. "Let's go for a drive."

"The street is hardly private," she pointed out. His reluctance to go upstairs with her was annoying.

"We'll find a quiet place," he assured her, and before she could protest further, he was leading her from the room.

"I still think my room would have been better," she insisted as he handed her up into his curricle. "I shall begin to think that you no longer find me attractive." Her voice was teasing, but the words were deadly serious.

She watched him with narrowed eyes as he silently climbed up into the carriage next to her and directed the horses out into the street. Perhaps he had not heard her question or felt that an answer was unnecessary. She would give him another chance.

"Why don't we drive down to the seaside?" Morgana suggested innocently. "It would be such fun to see some of our friends." And let them see Alex with her, she added to herself.

"Morgana, this is not a social call," Alex informed her curtly. He turned down a quiet road that led through a residential area to the edge of town. Once they were past all the houses, he pulled the carriage off the road and onto the grass.

Morgana watched him apprehensively. His unloverlike behavior had not gone unnoticed by her, and she could only think of two reasons for it. Either he was angry about the other night and intended to scold her, or he had decided to end their relationship. She was not ready for that to happen.

"You're angry about the other night at Nell Hardy's, aren't you?" she asked him, her manner penitent and suffering. "It was a terrible thing to do, but if you only knew how you hurt me, getting married like that . . ." She put her hand pleadingly on his arm and looked up into his face, her eyes filled with tears. "I won't do it again, darling."

He pulled his arm away. "For God's sake, Morgana, why all the drama? It's not as if we vowed eternal love," he snapped. "We both knew that it would end."

"But it doesn't have to," she cried. Damn, if he dropped her, she would be the laughingstock of Brighton. She would never live down the humiliation! "We can go on as we did before you were married." She let a few tears trickle down her cheeks.

Alex glanced at the fields around them, thankful that there was no one to overhear. Perhaps her room might have been better, for he could have walked out on her dramatics.

"This has nothing to do with my marriage or your behavior the other night," he told her impatiently. "I just want to end our relationship."

Morgana glared at him, becoming angry now. She had humbled herself, pleading with him to forgive her, but to no avail. "It's her, isn't it? She's making you stop seeing me."

"Who? Elizabeth? Of course not," he argued, but she barely heard him.

"She knows that as long as there's a real woman around, she'll never be able to hold you."

"Morgana, leave Elizabeth out of this!" he ordered.

"But I know you," she continued bitterly. "Even if I'm not there, she'll never keep you happy. She's not woman enough to satisfy you!"

"That's enough!" His voice was quiet but held a threat of violence. She stopped speaking as he flicked the reins and turned his horses onto the road back to town. "There's no point in talking about it," he snapped. "I had hoped to end this like reasonable adults, but you are making that impossible."

Reaching into his pocket, he pulled out the small box that contained her bracelet and tossed it into her lap. "I believe a gift is the customary way to conclude these affairs," he said coldly, not even bothering to look at her.

Morgana opened the box and took out the bracelet. She held it in her hand for a moment, then turned to him. "Is this supposed to make up for your treatment of me? Do you think I can be bought off with jewels?" Her voice quivered with outrage.

Alex glanced at her briefly as he turned onto another, slightly busier road. He was willing to risk the extra traffic in order to reach her inn more quickly. "Oh, I'm sure you'd love to throw that gaudy little bauble in my face," he said, laughing unpleasantly. "But I also know that you know how much it is worth. And you aren't about to throw away good jewels in a face-saving gesture!"

Morgana said nothing, only clutched the bracelet tightly in her hand. He was right, she knew, and hated him even more because of it. She stared ahead of them, her lips tightly compressed. She would make him pay, she vowed. She would make him . . .

A small group of people strolling along the beachfront walkway caught her eye. Morgana's face was suddenly lit by a smile.

"I have behaved very badly," she sighed penitently to Alex. "It came as quite a shock, you know, that you wanted to stop seeing me. But there are no hard feelings."

He glanced down at her, clearly skeptical, but she smiled sadly back up at him.

"The bracelet is lovely," she said with a sigh, holding it up to catch the light, then trying to put it on her wrist. The movement of the carriage made it impossible for her to clasp it. "Can you do it for me?" she asked politely. Seeing his frown, she quickly shook her head. "No, you don't have to do it. You haven't really forgiven me, and I understand." Her voice wavered pathetically.

"Oh, for goodness' sake, stop dithering. I'll hook the fool thing for you." With an exasperated sigh Alex pulled the carriage over to the side of the road. He took her wrist in his hand and bent over the clasp. Morgana glanced up. The people were coming closer, although they were talking together and had not noticed the carriage yet.

"There," he said impatiently as the bracelet was closed. He straightened up.

"Darling Alex," she sighed loudly. "Thank you so much for everything." Leaning forward, she slipped an arm around his neck and pulled him close for a kiss.

Alex jerked her arm away from his neck and pulled away from her. "Now what the devil was that for?" he snapped. Then, picking up the reins, he looked forward, directly into the astonished faces of his father, Margaret and Elizabeth.

CHAPTER ELEVEN

"I refuse to stay in the same house with him!" His Grace muttered. Not shocked into inaction as Elizabeth and Margaret had been, he had quickly led the two of them off the walkway and down onto the beach near the bathing machines. "His behavior is outrageous, and I, for one, do not intend to put up with it!"

"It isn't as if we didn't know about Morgana," Elizabeth pointed out quietly. "Why are you so upset?"

"And you aren't?" he snapped. Suddenly realizing where he was heading, he turned abruptly, and they walked along the sandy beach.

"I'm not pleased, I'll admit that, but I'm not—and neither are you—going to say anything to him about this!" Elizabeth insisted with quiet dignity.

His Grace stopped walking and turned to stare at her. "You mean you are going to ignore what we saw today?" he asked in disbelief.

"Yes," Elizabeth nodded. "I shall pretend that I saw nothing."

"But that's ridiculous!" His Grace cried, waving his arms about. "You can't just ignore it!"

"Sometimes it's all that you can do," Margaret said quietly, obviously quite shaken at seeing Alex with another woman.

His Grace turned to glare at her. "You know nothing about it," he snapped. "There's no sense in talking to you."

A middle-aged couple strolled past them, and they all nodded politely. An older woman accompanied by three young ladies giggling over the bathing machines also hurried by.

When they were safely away from the others, Margaret took a deep breath. "You are the one who knows nothing about it," she scolded His Grace. "You have never had to watch your husband obviously preferring other women to you."

He stopped and slowly turned to face her with a frown.

She paled slightly, but her voice was stern. "And no matter how angry you or I get, we must do as Elizabeth wants."

"And why is she the great authority?" he grumbled, glancing about to make sure they would not be overheard.

"She isn't," Margaret's voice was getting weaker as her courage ebbed away. "But she's the one who will have to live with the humiliation, not us, so we must give her the support she needs."

His Grace glared at her for a long moment, then shrugged his shoulders. "I think it's a mistake, but I'll do what you want. Just don't blame me when he flaunts her in our faces the next time we go out." He looked up toward the road. "If you ladies would like to wait here, I shall go find our carriage. I, for one, have had enough of the beach."

Only as he strode quickly away from them did Margaret let out her breath in a long sigh. She was trembling slightly as she took Elizabeth's arm.

"Thank you for persuading him," Elizabeth said quietly. "I don't think I could have borne another argument between them."

Margaret only smiled weakly. "I hope I don't have to do it too often or I shall have the vapors." She looked up at her daughter, her smile gone. "What I said wasn't true, though, Libby. Ignoring the situation isn't the only thing that you can do."

"I don't intend to start screaming at him. I know it would never change his mind," Elizabeth said with a frown.

"No," her mother said as she shook her head. "But you could leave." Elizabeth stared at her, so she went on. "We could go back to Welford, just the two of us. We could be happy there, and you wouldn't be faced with such humiliation and uncertainty."

"That seems like an awful extreme to go to," Elizabeth said quietly. "We've only been married a few weeks. I think it would be admitting failure if I ran back home. No," she said and shook her head slowly. "I have to learn to adjust."

"I was afraid you would say that," Margaret admitted. She stopped walking. "But you must promise me something. Promise that you'll keep it in mind. If things ever get intolerable, promise me that you'll come back home."

"Very well," Elizabeth said, and she forced herself to laugh. "But I can't imagine myself ever being ready to quit fighting."

Elizabeth saw His Grace waving to them from the carriage, and they turned toward him. As they walked toward him, Elizabeth noticed that two women walking near His Grace had stopped to greet him. Although they continued on their way quickly, they both turned back to gaze at him admiringly.

"You know," Elizabeth marveled, "Alex's father is very attractive. Was he so very much in love with his wife that he never considered remarrying up to this time?"

Margaret stopped walking and grabbed Elizabeth's arm, her face white with shock. "He's going to marry? Whom?"

"I didn't mean that he was planning it now," Elizabeth said as she turned to her mother. "Are you all right?" she cried, seeing her pallor.

Margaret nodded slowly. "It must be the sun," she said weakly.

Elizabeth gave her a strange look and held her arm as they walked up the slight incline to the carriage.

"I know of an excellent inn near here where we could have dinner," His Grace announced as he helped Elizabeth into the coach. He frowned at Margaret. "You look like you could use something to eat, too."

"But Alex . . ." Elizabeth protested.

He raised his eyebrows expressively. "I doubt Alex is rushing home at this moment, and if, by chance, he does, it would do him good to cool his heels awhile."

Elizabeth was not certain she agreed, but she was too dispirited to argue.

All Alex wanted to do was get home to see Elizabeth as quickly as possible, but the fates seemed against him. Once he had left Morgana at her inn, he hurried over to the jeweler's to get Elizabeth's necklace, but the store was closed, and it took several minutes before he was able to rouse someone from inside to help him. Then a wheel on his curricle cracked and broke, causing one of his horses to go lame. By the time he got the horses stabled and the crippled carriage to a smithy, it was getting late.

As the hackney he had hired ambled through the streets, Alex fretted restlessly inside. He would have proceeded faster if he had walked, he thought irritably.

In his mind he kept seeing Elizabeth's face as it

had been after Morgana had kissed him. He knew that his father and Margaret had been there also, but it was Elizabeth's hurt look that kept nagging at him. He had to tell her that it meant nothing, that Morgana was in the past, and she was his future. He fell back against the carriage wall in shock as he realized what he had been thinking. It was true, he suddenly knew. Elizabeth did mean far more to him than Morgana ever could, and it was because she was his wife that he no longer wanted any other woman. Good Lord! He had fallen in love with her!

It was so unexpected that Alex could do nothing but sit like a statue, staring blankly ahead of him. It was only when the carriage came to a jerking stop that he awoke from his daze and hurried out. He tossed some coins to the driver and raced up the stairs, feeling ridiculously happy. He could hardly wait to tell Elizabeth the news. Who could tell? Perhaps she cared about him, too!

The house was strangely quiet as he entered. With a frown he pushed open the door to the sitting room. It was empty. So were the library and the dining room. He hurried up the stairs and into Elizabeth's bedroom. It, too, was empty.

"Blast!" he muttered as he went slowly back down the stairs. "Where is everyone?" he asked the butler. "Did they go out for the evening?"

"They went out this afternoon, m'lord, and have not yet returned," the butler said. "Would m'lord like some dinner?"

Alex shrugged as he went into the library. "Just bring a tray in here," he said and walked across the room to pour himself a brandy. After taking a long drink he refilled the glass and glanced at the clock on the mantel. It was awfully late to be out for a drive, and they had not been dressed for any evening entertainment. Could something have happened to them? Surely they would have sent a message if their carriage had broken down, he tried to reassure himself. Besides, his father was along, and he would take care of them. Still he paced uneasily around the room until the butler entered with his dinner.

"Were there any messages for me?" Alex asked as soon as the butler had entered the room.

"No, m'lord," the man answered. "Shall I put your tray on the desk?"

Alex shrugged. "If you like," he muttered and poured himself some more brandy. Where could they be?

After two more brandies and about half of his dinner, Alex heard noises from the hallway. He dashed out of the library just as Elizabeth came up the stairs from the front door. His father and her mother were behind her.

A quick glance assured him that they had not been in some dire mishap. "Where have you been?" he snapped at them. "You should have been back hours ago!"

Elizabeth stopped short when she saw him, then continued up the stairs, a rather forced smile on her face. "Why, good evening, Alex," she said lightly. "We did not expect you would be home yet."

"I don't know why not," he cried angrily. "I would have told you if I were not going to eat dinner at home."

His father came the rest of the way up the stairs. "I took Elizabeth and her mother out to dinner." His look dared Alex to protest. "We ate at the Castle Inn."

"It was a delicious meal, too," Elizabeth added, ignoring the fact that all her food had tasted like sawdust and that she had had to fight an urge to burst into tears throughout the whole meal.

Alex looked unimpressed. "I would like to talk to you," he said, turning to Elizabeth.

"Now?" she gasped.

"But we were going to play a game of chess," Margaret came quickly to her daughter's rescue. "She promised that we could."

Alex tried unsuccessfully to hide his impatience. "I'm certain that my father would be happy to oblige you with a game," he told Margaret as he took Elizabeth's arm. "Right now I would like to talk to my wife."

Margaret smiled apologetically at Elizabeth and stood aside as Alex led her upstairs to her room.

"I think there is a chess set in the library," His Grace said to her. Then he turned to a footman. "Have the cook prepare some tea and bring it in to us," he said.

Margaret turned to stare at him. Did he really believe that she wanted to play chess now? Or could it be that he wanted some sort of distraction? She followed him into the library.

"Ah, here it is," he said as he pulled a box off a shelf. "We can play on that table over there." He nodded toward a small table cluttered with bric-a-brac.

She hurried over and began to clear it off while he moved two chairs over to it.

"Which do you prefer, black or white?" he asked as they sat down.

"It doesn't matter," she said with a shrug, listening for some sound from upstairs. "You don't suppose he would hurt her, do you?"

"Of course not," he snapped. "Here, you can be white."

She took her pieces and began to set them up on the board. "He was very angry," she reminded him quietly.

"He had no right to be," he said curtly.

Margaret bit her lip nervously and moved a pawn forward. "He seemed so polite in Welford," she whispered.

"I'm sure he was," he said sarcastically as he moved a knight.

She moved her pawn again and looked over at him timidly. "Were you angry that he married Elizabeth?"

"I thought we were playing chess," he said irritably. Moving his knight again, he captured her pawn.

Margaret said nothing but hurried to move her next piece. In her eagerness not to irritate him any further, though, her hand jerked and she knocked one of her rooks and a knight to the floor.

"Oh, I'm sorry," she murmured as she scrambled to the floor to retrieve her pieces before His Grace could move to help her. Still kneeling, she quickly put them back on the board and moved another pawn. Then she stood up, shook her skirt out slightly and sat back down.

His Grace was frowning at her. "Alex may be a fool, but he's not likely to beat her, you know."

Margaret nodded. "I know."

"Then what is the reason for your terror? What in the world do you think he's going to do?" he asked her, losing all patience.

"Nothing," she whispered.

His Grace sighed loudly. "If you aren't afraid of anything, then why do you jump every time I say anything to you?" His voice was rough with annoyance.

Margaret glanced up at him, then down at her hands, tightly clenched in her lap. "It's just that you seem to yell so much," she said hesitantly.

"Yell?" he cried loudly. "I do not yell!" He seemed to realize that perhaps he had been a trifle louder than necessary and coughed in embarrassment.

"That's just my manner," he explained. "You ought to know that I don't mean all the things I say."

"No, that's not true," Margaret said quickly, shaking her head. "When people are angry, that's when they say all the things they really mean. It's only when I get really upset that I have the courage to say what I really think."

"What rubbish!" he snapped, rising from his chair. She flinched back in her chair at his tone. "You make me sound like an ogre," he added, his eyes growing thoughtful as he watched her. "My God," he whispered. "You really believe that! You really believe that I meant all that rubbish!"

The look on his face made her uncomfortable, and she rose slowly to her feet. "I think I shall go up to my room now," she told him.

He ignored her remark. "Is that why you ran off with Timothy?" he asked in wonder.

She backed away from him slightly and tried to shrug off his question. "Goodness! That all happened so long ago, it's hard to remember." Her voice died away when she saw the determination on his face.

"But did you love him?" he demanded.

"He provided for us as best he could," she said weakly.

"Provided for you!" His Grace shouted. "If that's what you think love is, then you are more of a fool than I thought!"

Margaret's eyes widened. "I know what love is," she insisted with quiet dignity.

"I didn't mean that," His Grace said apologetically as he took a step toward her.

There was a quiet knock on the library door, and it opened. A footman wheeled in their tea. "Where would you like to serve the tea?" he asked politely.

"Oh, it doesn't matter." His Grace was not pleased with the interruption. He pointed to a low table before a sofa. "Over there would be fine."

The footman began to place the dishes on the table as Margaret edged nearer the door. "I don't think I'll have any tea," she said quietly to no one in particular.

His Grace spun around toward her. "I'm not finished, Margaret," he said sharply.

She glanced over at the footman, who had finished his task and was moving toward the door. "It has been such a long day." She looked his way as she spoke, her eyes filled with tears. "And I don't think I want to continue this discussion. Good night," she whispered quickly and fled out the door just before the footman.

"Margaret!" he shouted after her, but he knew she would not come back. "Hell and damnation!" he muttered and threw himself back into his chair. He saw the chess game still set up before him, and its presence irritated him excessively. With one quick swipe of his hand, he knocked all the pieces to the floor. Then he stared morosely at them. "Blast!" he whispered.

* * *

"Didn't it occur to you that I might wonder where you had all disappeared to? That I might even be worried when you didn't come home?" Alex said as he paced restlessly back and forth across Elizabeth's bedroom.

"No, it didn't," Elizabeth snapped. She had had enough today, and her resolution to remain calm was rapidly fading away. "Actually I never imagined that you'd be here."

Alex stopped walking and glared at her. "You needn't tell me—it was my father's idea to stay out late, wasn't it? I can just imagine him plotting a way to punish me for my imagined crimes. What the devil is he doing here, anyway?" he added.

Elizabeth sat down at her dressing table and began to remove the pins from her hair. She stopped at his question and turned toward him. "He didn't tell you?"

"My father and I do not spend much time chatting together," he pointed out sarcastically.

She turned back to her mirror. "Maybe that's why he's here—so you two can stop fighting for a change." She pulled a few more pins from her hair, then stopped and looked down at her hands. "No, that's not true," she said hesitantly. "He's here because he helped me out of a mess I found myself in while you were gone, and I rather forced him into moving in here to guide me."

"What sort of trouble?" he asked quietly.

She looked over at him. "I was stupidly trusting

again," she said with a shrug, "and his presence smoothed things over."

"Was Morgana involved?" His voice was cold.

Elizabeth bit her lip nervously. "I'm sorry, but she was."

Alex took a few steps closer. "Why the devil should you be sorry?" He was clearly puzzled.

"It must be hard for you to hear that she has done such things," Elizabeth said quietly. She knew that her face had become pale at the mention of Lady Tremayne's name, but she refused to ignore the subject.

Now Alex was really confused. "Why would it be hard? I never thought she was perfect."

"But if you care about her . . ."

"Where in the world do you get these strange ideas?" he cried. He moved over to the dressing table and pulled up a small stool. He sat down next to her and took one of her hands in his.

"You apparently are aware that Morgana and I have had a . . . um . . . relationship. Although it may shock you, I assure you that there is nothing very unusual about it," he told her quietly. He kept his eyes on her hand that he held, not on her face.

"I am aware that many married men see women other than their wives," she whispered.

He looked up and shook his head. "But I was not a married man when I was seeing Morgana," he pointed out. "And since I met you, I have not been with her. Do you understand what I am saying?" he asked.

She nodded her blushing face. "But you don't really need to explain."

"Damn it, yes I do," he exclaimed irritably. "You are thinking of what you saw today—I know you are—and you're doubting everything I'm saying." He took a deep breath. He continued, holding her eyes with his own. "Twice already Morgana has tried to cause trouble between us."

Elizabeth nodded slowly.

"That kiss you saw today was just another attempt to drive us apart. I was with her because she had some fool notion that I was going to marry her after her husband died, and I had to see her alone to make her understand that we were through."

"Did you want to marry her?" Elizabeth asked almost fearfully.

"I married you," Alex reminded her curtly.

"Yes, but if you had known that she was going to be free so soon afterward, would you have waited?" Elizabeth watched him closely, all her fears plainly written on her face.

He shook his head with a sigh. "I knew that her husband had died before I married you. Before I even asked you to marry me," he corrected. "I saw it in a newspaper while I was in Welford, and I could have hurried back to her if I had wanted to."

"Oh," Elizabeth whispered. She felt foolish for

doubting him and tried to pull her hand away, but he would not let her.

"Am I forgiven?" he teased.

"You didn't do anything wrong," she told him.

"I probably have done any number of things I ought to beg your forgiveness for." He laughed and brought her hand up to his lips. He kissed it slowly, then put it back into her lap. "I have something for you," he said, reaching into his pocket and pulling out the jeweler's box. He laid it on the table before Elizabeth.

She looked at him for a moment, then slowly opened the box. The string of pearls was lying on a bed of deep red velvet. "Oh, my!" she cried softly as she lifted out the necklace.

"I bought it at the same time as your earrings," he told her. "But the clasp was loose, so I couldn't give it to you then. I decided to wait and surprise you."

"I've never seen pearls this color," she murmured, uncomfortably aware that her suspicions about the relative values of her gift and Morgana's might have been wrong. "Are they very valuable?"

"Mercenary little thing, aren't you?" he teased as he took the necklace from her limp grasp. "Yes, a matched set of this length is rare, so they're probably worth more than some of the common stones. Lift your hair up so that I can put it on you," he ordered, for her hair had fallen into long curls down her back when she had taken the pins out.

She gathered the long tresses into her hands and

held them up so that he could slip the necklace around her neck and clasp it. She watched him in the mirror in front of her as he did so. "This day dress is not the proper setting for such lovely jewels," she laughed.

He looked up, meeting her eyes in the mirror. "You could take it off then," he suggested lightly.

She blushed and dragged her eyes from his to look at the necklace. "It's beautiful," she told him quietly.

"Yes," he whispered, and bent his head to kiss the nape of her neck.

Although she quivered inside, she did not move when his lips touched her. She closed her eyes and sat motionless as his lips moved along her neck to her ear. When his tongue tickled it gently, she sighed, totally unaware that her arms were slowly letting her hair fall.

By the time his lips reached hers, she was somehow wrapped tightly in his arms. His hands moved sensuously along her back, pushing her body closer and closer to him until she was incapable of any coherent thought except that she did not want him to stop.

"Oh, Libby," he sighed as his lips left hers. She was still held tightly in his arms, and his eyes looked down into her glowing face. "You don't know how worried I was after Morgana's trickery. I was so afraid that you would hate me."

Elizabeth turned slightly so that her face was resting against the rough material of his coat. She could feel his lips gently touching her hair. "No, I was hurt and a little angry, but I did not hate you." She pulled away from him slightly and looked up at his face with a smile. "But I did think you were remarkably stupid to prefer her to me," she teased. "After all, anyone can see that she doesn't love you."

"And you?" he asked.

Blushing faintly, the teasing look left her face, but she continued to gaze up at him. "While I do," she whispered and raised her lips to meet his. "Oh, how I do love you," she sighed.

He kissed her tenderly at first, but as he felt her arms go around his neck, his kiss deepened. Suddenly she felt his arms lifting her up, and he carried her across the room, placing her gently on the bed.

CHAPTER TWELVE

"I would really rather not go," Margaret told Elizabeth hesitantly. "You and Alex don't need me tagging along behind."

Elizabeth turned her head slightly so that her maid could continue to arrange her hair and frowned at her mother. "Don't be silly," she scolded. "The next thing you'll decide is that you want to go back to Welford."

"I had thought about it," Margaret admitted.

The finishing touches were added to Elizabeth's hair, and she stood up thankfully and hurried over to her mother's side. "Now what is all this about?" she asked quietly, picking up her mother's hand. Margaret was dressed in a lovely satin dress whose dusty blue color was particularly becoming to her. Her hair was softly curled and framed her face enchantingly, but her eyes were worried. "Why do you want to hurry back to Welford? What do you have back there? Both Alex and I want you to stay here as long as you'd like."

"But you and Alex don't seem to be having any problems now. I've never seen you happier than you've been this last week. You don't really need me here. Especially tonight at the Pavilion—I won't know anyone there but you two," she ended lamely.

"And His Grace," Elizabeth reminded her. Her maid held up the deep red dress she was to wear that evening, and Elizabeth walked away from her mother's side, allowing her maid to help her into it. She stood still as the girl buttoned the dress for her and then hurried into Elizabeth's dressing room.

Once her maid was out of the room, Elizabeth turned to her mother. "But I thought that you and Alex's father were getting along so much better," she said. "And at lunchtime he seemed quite eager to escort you."

"Did you think so?" Margaret asked timidly. She shook her head. "I'm sure he was just being polite, because he knew that my company was likely to be forced on him anyway."

"Oh, Mother," Elizabeth said with a sigh as her maid brought her shawl and shoes into the room. "If you really want to go home, I can't stop you, but do come with us tonight. Just think how you'll impress all your friends when you tell them you went to the Regent's Pavilion," she added.

Margaret shrugged her shoulders and sat down on the edge of the bed while Elizabeth looked at herself in the full-length mirror near the door. "Your dress is lovely," Margaret told her quietly.

"Yes, it is," Elizabeth said with a smile.

A knock was heard at the connecting door between hers and Alex's room, and it swung open. Alex walked in.

"My, we shall astound everyone with our loveliness tonight!" he said with an admiring glance at his wife and her mother. "Although a smile would help a little," he teased Margaret.

She forced a smile onto her face. "I had better find my reticule and shawl," she told him and hurried into the hallway, closely followed by the maid.

Alex walked over to Elizabeth's side. He took hold of both her hands, then stepped back slightly, holding her hands out so that he could see her dress. "You look beautiful," Alex said, his eyes roaming over her with approval.

"Thank you," she whispered. She blushed slightly but did not turn away.

Alex pulled her into his arms and kissed her gently on the lips. "Wouldn't it be more fun to stay home?" he teased.

"Oh, not you too!" Elizabeth shook her head. "Why is it that no one else wants to see the Pavilion as much as I do?"

Alex laughed, walked over to her dressing table and picked up her pearl necklace. "And who else does not want to go? Your mother?" He moved behind her and put the necklace around her neck.

"I think your father makes her nervous," Elizabeth said, and she sighed. "She decided it would be easier to stay home than to spend time with him."

"Is that why she was so eager to go shopping with you today rather than stay home?" he asked as he clasped the necklace. He kissed her neck lingeringly. "Did you promise we would protect her from my cruel and wicked father?" He laughed, turning her around in his arms and kissing her again. "I really would rather stay home," he whispered as he leered at her.

Elizabeth wiggled out of his hold. "You may if you like, but I am going." She picked up her shawl and reticule and walked to the door. Her face was solemn, but her eyes were twinkling.

Alex sighed and opened the door for her. "We'll go, but don't blame me if the evening is a dead bore."

Elizabeth later wondered how any evening spent in such splendor could possibly be a dead bore. The Pavilion far surpassed anything she could have imagined. She had heard, of course, of the Chinese Gothic Music Room and the silver dragons, but she was not prepared for the huge chandeliers hissing with the new gaslights. Nor had she ever imagined the way the walls were decorated with mandarins and fluted yellow draperies to resemble Chinese tents. The ceilings were a peach-blossom color, and canopies of tassels and bells were everywhere. The five-clawed silver dragons she had read about darted from every chandelier and overmantel until she began to suspect that they were alive and that the house was overrun by them.

"I suspect the Regent admires Chinese artifacts," Elizabeth whispered to Alex.

His lips twitched slightly. "He had wanted the newer addition built like a Chinese pagoda, but his architects dissuaded him. Actually this gallery was built because he had received a gift of some Chinese wallpaper and wanted a place to hang it."

"All this for wallpaper?" Margaret whispered as she glanced at the outrageously furnished room.

"The kitchens are said to be models of efficiency," His Grace felt required to point out.

"Are they Chinese also?" Elizabeth said with a laugh.

"I doubt that Prinny ever goes in them, so they wouldn't need to be," Alex said with a grin. "All he cares about is what comes out of them."

As they were laughing, a quietly dressed, middle-aged man came hurrying up to them. "Margaret Corbett?" he cried. "Is it really you?"

Margaret looked at him in surprise, a sudden smile lighting up her face. "Mr. Loring," she said. "What a delightful surprise!"

"Do you realize that after all these years, you still owe me a dance?" he teased. "I insist that you come with me to the ballroom and pay your debt!"

His Grace glowered at the man, but Mr. Loring only had eyes for Margaret. "Mrs. Corbett is here with us," His Grace said forbiddingly.

"I would be happy to dance with you," Margaret said as if His Grace had not spoken. She took the man's arm and allowed him to lead her through the crowd, relieved to be away from His Grace's probing eyes. With any luck she could have a short but pleasant visit with Elizabeth and Alex, and Gerald would never learn of her feelings for him.

His Grace watched them disappear, then, muttering something about finding some acquaintances of his own, he left.

"We seem to be on our own now," Alex said quietly. "Would you like to dance or find something to eat?"

"Oh, let's dance," Elizabeth cried. "That sounds much more enjoyable."

"My thoughts entirely," Alex murmured, and he led her into the next room.

The Prince Regent seemed to believe that a lot of something was good but to have it to excess was best of all. This not only applied to the decorating of his houses but to the number of people he invited to his parties. There was such a crowd that it was impossible to greet or even see everyone who was there.

Elizabeth had been dancing with Alex for more than an hour before she noticed a familiar face across the room. She stiffened involuntarily in Alex's arms.

"What's wrong?" he asked with a frown of concern.

"Nothing." Elizabeth tried to laugh it off, but she

could not help glancing back across the room again. Alex followed her gaze.

"Morgana," he muttered, then looked down at Elizabeth. "We are bound to see her occasionally. She frequents some of the same circles we do."

Elizabeth nodded. "Yes, I know. It's just that I had forgotten about her for a while." She smiled up at him, but her eyes held a hint of worry.

Alex squeezed her. "Forget about her again, then," he ordered lightly. "She is nothing to either of us."

Elizabeth remembered Alex's remark later when he had gone to get them both a glass of punch. It was true, she smiled to herself. Morgana could do nothing to hurt them. She was part of the past.

A couple vacated a sofa near her, and she walked over to sit down, grateful for the chance to rest her feet. Once she was seated, she looked around curiously, realizing that the Pavilion was not the place of wealth and beauty that she had imagined it would be but a garish monstrosity instead. A writhing golden dragon with glittering red eyes peered down at her from its perch on a nearby pedestal. Elizabeth shuddered and turned to look the other way.

This time she was facing a dragon of a different sort, she thought with a smile as she spotted Morgana sitting with a group of her friends not far away. Several gentlemen seemed desirous of her company, for there was a constant parade of them to her side.

Morgana appeared to be so busy flirting with them that she had not noticed Elizabeth sitting there.

Elizabeth watched them with interest. Now that Alex was no longer caught in Morgana's trap, Elizabeth was mildly intrigued by Lady Tremayne's methods. Two young gentlemen came over to her, obviously begging for some favor. She merely laughed, playing them off against each other until Elizabeth suspected that they would become furious and stomp away. Instead they joined the crowd sitting around Morgana, glaring angrily at the other men.

The next gentleman to seek out Morgana was none other than Sir Quentin Paine. Elizabeth felt uneasy and slid back slightly in her seat, hoping he would not notice her. There was little chance that he would, however, for he only had eyes for Morgana. He abruptly ordered one young man to move and sat down next to Lady Tremayne, engaging her in conversation to the exclusion of all others.

Morgana seemed to favor Sir Quentin, for she also ignored the other men. Elizabeth was beginning to get bored and was about to turn to watch for Alex when Morgana raised one arm gracefully, and the light caught the bracelet she was wearing. Elizabeth recognized it with a gasp. It was the one Alex had bought for Morgana, the one whose diamonds Elizabeth had taken!

Elizabeth could not have turned away if she had wanted to. She was frozen in horror as she watched

Morgana preen over the bracelet. Some of the men with her only glanced at it briefly, angry, perhaps, that she was wearing a gift from someone else. Sir Quentin, though, did not dismiss it as quickly as the others. He must have asked to see it, for Morgana proudly held her arm out to him. He fingered the bracelet slowly, sliding it about her dainty wrist.

Although she could not see his face when he looked up and spoke to Morgana, Elizabeth did see Lady Tremayne's. It grew dark with anger, and she swiftly pulled her arm back. Sir Quentin turned slightly, and Elizabeth could see him laughing quietly. He must have said something to the other men there, for a few of the more brave ones began to snicker, while the others looked uneasy.

Oh my, Elizabeth thought, did they know there were paste stones in the bracelet? She had not been able to tell the difference, but that did not mean someone more experienced with jewels would not be able to. She felt her mouth go dry with fear. Would Morgana say something to Alex? What would happen to their newfound happiness if he discovered what she had done?

Almost as if Morgana could sense her fear in the air, she looked straight across the room to Elizabeth. There was pure hatred in her eyes, and something else even more frightening. She knew! Morgana knew that Elizabeth was responsible for the paste stones!

Saying nothing to the people around her, Morgana

rose to her feet and walked around the groups of laughing people, straight to Elizabeth.

"I would like to speak to you," she said with deadly quiet.

Elizabeth tried to smile. "I don't believe I have anything to say to you," she replied with false bravado.

Morgana was not impressed. She glanced at the people around them. Elizabeth was uneasily aware that they were attracting some attention. "I don't think you want to talk here," Morgana noted with meaning.

Desperately trying to hold onto her dignity, Elizabeth rose to her feet. She did not want to talk to Morgana here or anywhere, but she recognized the determination in her face. "Very well," Elizabeth said coldly. "I trust you know of a more private place?"

Morgana nodded and turned around, weaving her way quickly through the crowds toward a door in the far wall. Elizabeth followed her more slowly, desperately wishing that the floor would swallow her up.

The floor refused to cooperate, however, and Elizabeth found herself in the hallway, face to face with a very angry Morgana.

"This way," Morgana snapped, and she turned down another hallway. There were fewer people around.

Morgana stopped in front of a door and pushed it

open. A couple on the sofa jumped apart guiltily as she walked into the room.

"Why, Isabella Hartnett!" Morgana cried in mocking concern. "I do believe your father was looking for you!"

The young man paled slightly and muttered something to Isabella. Then they both hurried out of the room, barely noticing Elizabeth as she stood by the door.

Morgana walked into the center of the room and turned back to Elizabeth, waiting impatiently as she stepped slowly into the room and closed the door behind her.

"I certainly underestimated you," Morgana said softly, not bothering to hide her animosity. "But I never dreamed you'd be so foolish as to try to fight back."

"I'm afraid I don't know what you are talking about," Elizabeth said coldly. She walked further into the room, pretending an interest in an elaborate silken tapestry, although she was quaking with terror inside.

"You may trick Alex with that innocent act," Morgana hissed, "but I'm no fool. I know you were responsible for the paste stones in my bracelet."

"Paste stones?" Elizabeth turned toward Morgana, feigning surprise. "Why on earth should you suspect me? Wouldn't it be more logical that your jeweler cheated you?"

Morgana took a few steps closer. "I did not buy

this myself, as you very well know. It was a gift—a gift from your husband. To show the depth of his feelings for me."

A smile broke out involuntarily on Elizabeth's lips. "Perhaps the paste stones are a measure of his feelings," she said with a laugh.

Morgana did not share her humor. "You caused me to be humiliated before all my friends. I shall ruin you for it," she cried, her eyes flashing angrily.

"I believe you've already tried that," Elizabeth noted, finding it difficult to control her growing anger.

"Those pitiful attempts were nothing," Morgana snapped. She clutched the back of a chair tightly. "I shall make you sorry that you ever dared tangle with me!"

"I already am sorry that I ever met you," Elizabeth noted dryly. "And as much as I've enjoyed our little chat, I think I shall go." She turned toward the door.

"Just a moment!" Morgana reached the door before Elizabeth. "I'm not some servant to be dismissed whenever it pleases you. It makes me laugh the way you strut around, as if being Lady Waring made you better than the rest of us!"

"That's not true," Elizabeth argued.

"Why, everybody who looks at you knows that you'll never keep Alex satisfied. He'll start looking for a real woman soon. I've even heard that bets are

217

being placed on how long it will take," she added slyly.

"What rubbish!" Elizabeth exclaimed. "As if people in London have nothing else to do but wait for my marriage to fail."

Morgana smiled unpleasantly. "Oh, but you underestimate your appeal, my dear. You see, no one in town can understand why Alex married you, so there is a great deal of speculation. Perhaps I ought to end their suspense and tell them."

"What do you know about my marriage?" Elizabeth tried to sound self-confident but failed under Morgana's triumphant gaze.

Alex carefully carried two cups of some innocuous punch around the edge of the ballroom, searching for Elizabeth. He remembered leaving her somewhere near that hideous golden dragon, but she was nowhere to be seen. He sighed as he put the two cups down on a small table and looked more carefully at the couples dancing. Had someone asked her to dance while he was gone?

As he peered at the crowd, he felt a light tap on his arm. It was not Elizabeth, as he had suspected, but his friend Denby.

"Quite a squeeze, isn't it?" he said to his friend.

Denby did not even bother to answer. "A storm is rolling up fast, old boy," he warned.

Alex stared at him.

"Lady Tremayne just sailed by, spitting fire, and she had your wife in tow," he clarified.

"Elizabeth and Morgana?" Alex gasped.

Denby nodded. "And they weren't going to discuss what to get you for your birthday."

Alex looked around him quickly, as if he expected to see them exchanging fisticuffs in a corner. "Where did they go?" he asked frantically.

Denby nodded toward a door across the ballroom. "I followed them though that door, then I got waylaid by an old friend of my mother's. There are some small parlors down that way."

"Thanks," Alex said quietly, shaking his friend's hand. Then he hurried around the room to the door Denby had pointed out.

It seemed there were hundreds of people milling about in the hallway outside the ballroom. He pushed his way through them and opened a door in the far wall. It was a storage closet.

Ignoring the strange looks he received, he hurried over to another door that he had spotted. It wasn't even closed, for the dozen or so men inside playing cards had nothing to hide. They looked up in surprise at Alex's sudden entrance. He smiled weakly at them and backed quickly out of the room.

A quieter hallway turned down another way, and Alex hurried down it. The first room he tried held an ardently embracing couple. They broke apart as he opened the door.

"Oh, Lord Waring," the girl smiled invitingly.

"Good evening, Isabella," he said curtly and, turning, left the room.

The next room held an elderly lady reclining on a sofa. She screamed faintly as Alex pushed open the door.

"Excuse me," he muttered and quickly closed the door.

Standing in the hallway, Alex looked about him. Where could they be?

There was another door off the hallway, and Alex trudged toward it without much hope. They must have gone down some other hallway. He pushed the last door open and found Morgana and Elizabeth staring back at him.

Nodding politely to Morgana, Alex turned to his wife. "If you are ready to leave, my dear, I really think we had best get back to the ballroom."

Elizabeth took a step toward him, but Morgana was quicker. "Oh, no," she cried, rushing between Alex and Elizabeth. "She's not going to hurry out of here with you. Not after what she did to me!"

Alex flashed Elizabeth a reassuring smile. "And just what terrible thing did she do to you?" he asked cynically.

Morgana's eyes narrowed. "You needn't be so self-righteous," she snapped at Alex. "Her actions do not reflect well on you."

Alex sighed impatiently. "Come now, Morgana. I am tired of your games. Say what you have to say or we shall leave." He saw Elizabeth's worried look and, walking over to her side, he took her hand.

His action further angered Morgana. "Oh, yes, go protect your precious little wife," she sneered. "You've already decided that she's such an innocent and that I'm just lying, haven't you?" She whipped off her bracelet and held it up in front of her. "If that's true, why then did she put paste stones in my bracelet? There are six paste stones and not one diamond!"

Alex did not cry out indignantly or draw back from Elizabeth in disgust as she feared he might do. Instead, he burst into laughter.

"You expect me to believe that?" he laughed. "And what makes you think those stones are paste?"

"I doubt that Sir Quentin could crack a real diamond," she said.

Alex shrugged his shoulders. "There were diamonds in there when it was bought. It might be more appropriate to question your staff about it than my wife." He turned to Elizabeth. "Come, my dear," he said, and started to lead her toward the door.

"How convenient for her that you trust her so implicitly," Morgana sneered at them. "I wonder if she trusts you so completely."

Alex stopped walking and turned toward her.

"Of course I trust him," Elizabeth said quietly. She took a step toward Morgana, facing her with dignified courage. "And if you mean to shock me with news of your relationship with him, it won't work. I happen to know that it is in the past."

"So he confessed everything to you, did he?" Morgana said with a laugh, but it had a cruel sound to it. "And you have forgiven him, of course."

"There was nothing to forgive," Elizabeth noted. "It was in the past, before we were married."

"Elizabeth," Alex called softly, for he could see the signs of Morgana's rage, but she did not appear to hear him.

"And when he was confessing all this," Morgana continued with a sudden smile, "did he also tell you that it was my idea that he marry you? That he only did it to anger his father, who hates you? That we considered it a great joke and laughed about it for hours?"

"I don't believe you," Elizabeth cried out. She spun around to look at Alex. Her face was pale and her eyes were round with fear. "It isn't true, is it?" she whispered.

Alex stared at her, not knowing what to tell her.

"Yes, Alex," Morgana laughed, seeing his indecision. "Tell her it isn't true. Let's see how you can convince her that it wasn't all just a joke that I suggested." Her eyes glinted maliciously.

"Damn it, get out of here!" Alex shouted at Morgana. The look in his eyes must have convinced her that she had gone too far this time. He watched her scurry from the room, then turned back to Elizabeth. "Let's go," he suggested quietly. "We can talk about this later." He reached for her arm, but she drew back from his touch.

"No," Elizabeth cried, shaking her head. "No, we'll talk about it now." Her face was deathly pale as she backed away from him, a horrid pain raging through her. "It's true, isn't it?" she whispered hoarsely. "But of course, it's true!" She put her hand up to her mouth and turned away as if it hurt her too much to see him.

Alex took a step toward her, then stopped as he saw her recoil. "It's not as it sounds," he pleaded.

"What a fool I was not to realize it myself!" Elizabeth said as if she was in a daze. "It explains everything—your father's terrible anger, your strange behavior, the frantic way you remade me so that I'd be presentable."

"Elizabeth, stop it!" he cried, striding angrily over to her. He grasped her by the shoulders and turned her to face him. "That's not how it was!"

Elizabeth turned to look at him, feeling unutterably weary. "Are you denying everything she said? That you married me for some reason besides a desire to anger your father? Perhaps I am a little bird-witted, but it seems rather unbelievable. Surely you must have had less drastic ways of angering your father."

"I wish I could deny everything," he said sadly, "but the truth is that my father became very angry at me and ordered me to marry within three months. I was furious, and determined to thwart him."

"And if you did not obey?"

"He was going to leave all his unentailed property to you, as his only other relative," Alex told her quietly.

"Even though he hated me?"

"Yes," Alex whispered. "He was very angry with me at the time."

"I know I did not make a good impression on your father the first time I met him, but I can't understand why you each felt you could just use me as a tool to hurt the other one," she said.

Alex winced at her words. "Neither of us can be proud of our actions, but mine were far worse," he admitted. "I had decided before I ever reached Welford that I was going to marry you even though I knew nothing about you. Knowing what my father's reaction to our wedding would be was enough for me. Once we were married, though, things changed," he added quickly.

"Oh, of course," Elizabeth agreed sarcastically. "From being the despised cousin, I became the beloved wife. I'm sorry, but I've lost my liking for fairy stories tonight."

Taking a deep breath, she walked a few steps away from him. Her head was bowed and her hands were tightly clenched in front of her as she tried to hide her deep hurt. Suddenly she straightened up and spun around, laughing slightly as she saw his concerned face. "Oh, you mustn't think it really matters why you married me." She pasted a bright smile on her face. "After all, it wasn't as if we married for love. Goodness knows, I certainly didn't." She giggled slightly at his frown. "Well, perhaps for the love of all your money."

"Elizabeth! For God's sake, stop!" Alex cried.

"I will admit, though, that Morgana was right," she continued determinedly. "I did put the paste stones in her bracelet. Not that I cared the slightest bit that you had a mistress, but she behaved so vulgarly about it. I thought she needed to be taught her place."

"Morgana's only trying to throw a rub in the way," Alex tried to reason with her. "Don't let her succeed."

"Haven't you been listening?" Elizabeth laughed. "If I'm willing to admit that I married you because you are wealthy, why should I care if you married me to anger your father?" By this time she realized that her laughter had a hysterical sound to it, but it was either laugh or cry, and her pride would not let her cry in front of him.

"You're upset," Alex said softly. "Don't say these things. You know you don't mean them."

"How would you know what I mean or don't mean?" she lashed out at him. Tears were forming in the corners of her eyes, and she turned around for a minute, blinking them away rapidly. She would not humble herself completely.

"But what I said is true," she insisted, turning back to face him. Her voice was becoming weaker, for she was losing the battle to control her battered emotions. The pain was almost more than she could bear, and her eyes were stinging from holding back the tears. "I'm no fool." She tried to laugh, but her voice cracked. "I like expensive clothes, good food, coming to wonderful places like this." Her hand waved vaguely around her as Alex swam for a moment before her eyes. "Why, I would have married your father if he had offered," she added.

Tears blurred her vision again, and when she could see again, Alex was right before her. "Please let me take you home, Elizabeth," he whispered.

"And miss the rest of the party?" She pulled away from him. Tears were streaming down her face, but she kept up her cheerful charade. "Actually, I had better get back to the ballroom. I'm sure I've promised this dance to someone." With a bright smile that looked ridiculous amid her tears, she fled from the room.

She had no desire to return to the ballroom but hurried down the hallway in the opposite direction. She did not care where it led as long as it was away from everyone.

She had wondered why Alex had come to Welford and why he had wanted to marry her, but she could never have thought of a reason as horrid as the truth. What a fool she had been! While he was trying to anger his father, she was confessing her love for him!

"Elizabeth!" She spun around to see Alex hurrying along the corridor behind her.

Suddenly panicking, Elizabeth turned a corner. The tears were flowing more heavily now, and she could barely see as she pushed past a crowd of people laughing and talking. She rushed through a door and found herself outside.

Wiping the tears from her cheeks with the back of her hand, she looked around in surprise. She was on a terrace of some sort that was lit with only an occasional candle. Certain that she could hear Alex's footsteps coming up close behind her, she darted down a stone path that meandered under some trees.

Elizabeth had no real thought of where she was going, just a desperate need to be alone. The blackness of the night cloaked her from the curious eyes that always seemed to be watching. It also somehow seeped into her mind to soothe it with blessed numbness. The tears stopped slowly, and her desperate race became a walk.

She was only vaguely aware of the people she was passing, her mind seeing them as mere objects to walk around, not as individuals who might intrude into her trance. When someone took her arm and pulled her to a stop, she was astonished.

"And who have we here?" a slightly slurred male voice asked. He leaned forward so that his face was only inches from hers. Elizabeth stared blankly at him.

"Were ya out here lookin' fer us?" another man asked with a laugh.

Elizabeth turned toward the second voice, but she

could see no more than just his dim outline. "No, I wasn't," she whispered uncertainly, trying to pull her arm away.

"Oh, the poor lass weren't looking fer us," the first man mocked. "Now ain't that just a shame, 'cause we was looking fer you!" he added, letting his fingers caress her arm.

"Don't be shy, lass," the other man said, seeing her shudder. "We only want a bit of fun." He moved closer to her.

"Please let me go," she said impatiently.

"No, we couldn't do that," he said. His hand reached out to turn her face toward him. "A pretty thing like yerself shouldn't be out here alone. No tellin' who ya might meet!" His hold loosened slightly as he laughed.

Elizabeth had had enough. She had been hurt—devastated—by the things she had learned, and her first reaction had been to run away, to hide somewhere, to lick her wounds in private. But that desire was gone, and in its place was a raging anger and a need to strike out at someone, to hurt as she had been hurt. These fools were too convenient to be ignored.

As they laughed at their wit, Elizabeth moved her head slightly so that the man's hand was right below her mouth. She opened it wide and without warning sank her teeth into his hand.

The man screamed out in surprise and pain. "Why, you little slut!" he cried, but from a safer distance.

Elizabeth quickly aimed her foot at the other man's shins and boxed his ears at the same time. His yells of pain were music to her ears, and she experienced a shocking desire to hit him again.

Her intent must have been evident to the two men, for they did not wait for her next moves. With muttered complaints about unladylike behavior, they hurried into the darkness.

Elizabeth looked around her, feeling tired but strangely calm. She spotted a bench in the shadows hidden by some overgrown bushes and dragged herself over to it. She sat down with a long sigh, knowing suddenly what she wanted to do. She wanted to go home.

The sound of footsteps on the stone path caused her to stiffen in anticipation.

"Elizabeth!" she heard Alex call softly.

After a moment she saw him approaching along the path. She could have called out to him or made some noise to tell him where she was, but, in truth, she had no desire to talk to him. What was there left to say?

She sat deathly still, thankful that her dress was dark and would be hard to spot. Once he had moved on, she breathed a sigh of relief and stood up. She did not know how far down the path Alex would go, but he would most likely come back this way, and she did not want to give him another chance to spot her. She hurried down the path in the other direction, to the house.

Her absence had certainly not been noticed, for she slipped easily back into the house and wandered through the crowd. She carefully kept her face down, knowing that her cheeks must be streaked with tears. All she hoped to do was find her mother and ask her to go home with her.

Reaching the ballroom door, Elizabeth risked a glance around the room. She spotted her mother very quickly, but she was with His Grace and another, older man with wispy bits of gray hair. It would cause too much attention if she were to interrupt them now, she realized with a disappointed sigh. She turned away from the door when she felt a light touch on her arm.

Oh God! Alex had found her, she thought, and her body stiffened. She turned slowly. Sir Matthew Denby was at her side. She smiled at him in vague relief.

"Lady Waring, are you all right?" he asked quietly.

Elizabeth fought back a desire to giggle, for his question seemed absurd after all she had been through this evening. "Yes." She nodded, then stopped. "No, actually I'm not," she admitted quietly. Glancing around quickly, she pulled him gently back into the hallway.

"I desperately want to go home," she told him, her face alarmingly pale. "Do you think you could help me?"

"Of course," he cried, embarrassed by her distress.

"Let me find Alex for you." He started to turn away, but she grabbed his arm.

"No!" she whispered hoarsely. He looked at her strangely, and she closed her eyes for a moment. She forced herself to appear calmer when she opened her eyes again. "No, I would rather if you just took me home or called a carriage for me," she said quietly.

"I couldn't send you in a carriage by yourself," Denby protested uncertainly. Her pain was plainly visible to him and to anyone else who happened to look at her. Whatever had happened with Lady Tremayne must have been awful, he thought with a wave of sympathy for his friend's wife. He would take care of her, make certain that she got home safely, and then he would come back and find Alex.

"I think this hallway will take us around to the front entrance," he said, taking her hand. She smiled at him gratefully as he led her purposefully through the crowd.

CHAPTER THIRTEEN

Alex found his father in the ballroom, glowering at the dancing couples.

"Have you seen Elizabeth? Where is Margaret?" Alex asked, looking around him quickly.

His father nodded toward the dance floor. "Margaret's out there with some fool named Mowery. Another of her former beaux. Brighton appears to be filled with them," he complained as he glanced over at his son. When he saw that Alex had barely heard his lament, a worried look crossed his face. "I haven't seen Elizabeth. Is something wrong?"

Alex nodded, stopping his perusal of the dance floor long enough to glance at hs father.

"Don't tell me." His Grace's lips narrowed in irritation. "What did Morgana do this time?"

With a quick glance around him, Alex leaned closer to his father. "She told Elizabeth the real reason I married her," he said quietly.

"The devil!" His Grace breathed. He reached out

and took hold of Alex's arm. "And Elizabeth, how is she?" His concern showed clearly on his face.

"How would you expect?" Alex snapped, but his bitterness was not aimed at his father but at himself. "Quite understandably, she wants nothing to do with me. She ran off someplace, and I haven't seen her for almost an hour now. I thought maybe Margaret would have seen her."

His Grace nodded. "The fool set is almost over."

They waited in silence together, occasionally nodding to acquaintances. The last minutes of the set seemed interminably long, but finally Margaret was brought back to where they stood by her balding partner.

"I hope I might have the honor of another dance later this evening," Mr. Mowery said to her.

"We shan't be here later," His Grace snapped, and he frowned at the man until he hurried away.

"What's wrong?" Margaret asked as His Grace took her arm and led her toward the door.

"Have you seen Elizabeth?" Alex asked her.

She shook her head. "No, not since she was dancing with you. She isn't lost, surely, is she?" Glancing back into the crowded ballroom, Margaret said, "She is probably just dancing with someone."

"No, it's more than that," Alex frowned. "We had words, and I'm afraid she was quite upset."

Margaret looked from Alex's concerned face to his father's. "She must be here somewhere," she whispered fearfully. "Have you checked everywhere?"

"There are so many damned people here," Alex muttered, then remembered Margaret's presence. "Sorry," he muttered.

Margaret waved off his apology as someone hurried up behind them. "Mrs. Corbett," someone called.

They all turned to see Denby joining them. "Mrs. Corbett," he repeated. "Lady Waring asked me to tell you that she has gone home."

"Elizabeth?" Alex asked quickly. "She's all right?"

Denby nodded. "Didn't give me any message for you, though," he said with embarrassment. "Just the one for her mother."

"But she was all right?" Alex persisted.

Denby looked at Margaret and Alex's father as if wondering how much to say in front of them.

"For God's sake, man, we know she was upset," His Grace snapped impatiently.

"That she was," Denby agreed. "But I don't think anyone noticed. I took her out a side door, and no one stopped to talk to her."

"Thanks, old pal," Alex said with a sigh. "Thank God she found someone she could trust."

When they finally arrived home, Margaret found her daughter restlessly pacing her bedroom. "At last," Elizabeth cried when her mother came into the room. "I thought you were never going to get here."

She stopped and looked suspiciously at her mother. "Did *they* come with you?"

"If you mean Alex and Gerald, yes, they did," Margaret said. She took off her shawl and tossed it onto the bed. Then she sat down on the chair before Elizabeth's dressing table, turning her seat so that she could see her daughter. "Now would you please tell me just what happened? Those two downstairs would tell me nothing."

Elizabeth ignored her question. She came over and sank to her knees before her mother, holding one of her hands tightly. "I want to go home," she said.

"Home?" Margaret was puzzled. "But . . ."

"Home to Welford," Elizabeth said quickly. "You said I would always have a place there with you."

"Yes, but that was before. I thought that you and Alex . . ."

Elizabeth stood up and turned away. "I don't belong here," she said bitterly. "I was a fool to think I ever would."

Margaret put her hand on Elizabeth's arm. "But Alex is so fond of you," she said softly. "He'll help you adjust; and Gerald admires you, too. I can tell."

"Oh, Mother, if you only knew how funny that was," Elizabeth said ironically. "Do you know why Alex married me?"

"Because he loved you, I thought," she said weakly. "He certainly acted as if he did."

Elizabeth smiled cynically. "Because his father ordered him to marry in three months or he would leave his fortune to me—even though he readily admitted that he hated me—since I was his only other relative. Alex decided that as his bride, I would be the perfect revenge!"

Margaret was very pale. "Oh, no, Libby, Alex would not do that!"

"Mother!" Elizabeth said sharply. "Whom do you think told me? He not only admitted it was true but he also filled in the missing details for me."

"Oh, Libby," her mother protested. "He seemed so trustworthy."

Elizabeth shrugged her shoulders and gently removed her mother's hand from her arm. "So you can see why I am not staying here any longer than I have to." She walked over to her wardrobe and pulled down a small valise. "Are you coming with me?"

Margaret nodded slowly and watched her daughter bustle about the room. I certainly have acted like a prize fool these last few days, she silently scolded herself. "Maybe you are right," she said aloud to her daughter. "I don't think either of us belongs here."

"We'll only take a few things with us, and they can send the rest later," Elizabeth said as she pulled a nightdress from her closet and, folding it, put it on her bed. She added some underthings and one of her old dresses to the pile. "Get your things and bring them in here. It will be easier if we only have one bag to manage."

"You want to go tonight?" Margaret asked in surprise. "Why not sleep here and leave in the morning?"

"After the way both of them have humiliated us?" Elizabeth cried. "I would rather sleep in the street than under the same roof as either Alex or his father!"

Elizabeth threw open the valise and picked up her pile of clothing. She stopped suddenly as she glanced into the bag. Putting the clothes back down on the bed, she reached inside the case and pulled out a dusty old box. "This certainly can stay here!" she insisted and tossed it onto the bed. The box fell open, and the Herriad Necklace spilled onto the coverlet.

After she had stuffed all her clothes into the bag, she grabbed the necklace and hurried over to the desk in the corner of the room. She pulled out a piece of paper and opened the bottle of ink.

"This fool necklace is all they ever really wanted anyway, so they should be delighted to get it back," she announced, too angry and hurt to be rational.

"But I thought you said no one ever mentioned it," Margaret pointed out.

"They were trying to be clever," Elizabeth scoffed, and she began to write very quickly. "You had better get your things," she reminded her mother.

Margaret nodded and hurried across to her own room.

CHAPTER FOURTEEN

Alex poured out two glasses of brandy, one for his father and one for himself. His Grace carried his glass across the room and sat down heavily in a large upholstered chair. He took a sip of the liquor and put the glass down on a table next to him.

His son remained by the liquor cabinet. In one long drink he finished his first brandy and then poured himself another generous one. "What can they be doing all this time?" he said impatiently. "I should have gone up there myself instead of listening to Margaret. She's my wife, after all; she would have listened to me."

"Oh, no doubt," his father murmured sarcastically. "You have such finesse and tact. That must be why she ran back here rather than let you escort her."

Alex walked to the door and pulled it open, looking anxiously up the empty stairway. He closed the door slowly with a sigh, sat down on a nearby chair and stared moodily in front of himself.

His father watched him silently for a moment. "Do you love her?" he asked suddenly.

"Of course," Alex cried, looking up defiantly. "And you needn't bring up all that nonsense you said at Herriaton about her gambling away your fortune or her unsuitability. None of it is true."

"I know that," His Grace said easily. "I wondered if you did." He looked hard and long at his son. "She's much more than you deserve, you know. You acted reprehensibly in marrying her the way you did, but if she loves you, you have a chance of winning her forgiveness. Does she?" he asked quietly.

Alex looked concerned. "She said she married me for my money," he admitted.

His father only laughed. "She said that tonight, I'll wager. No, I would find that hard to believe. She was much too upset over Morgana to have married you for such a practical reason."

"You mean tonight?"

"No," His Grace said, and he shook his head. "While you went after Margaret, Elizabeth and I had a long talk. Once she was convinced that you were not in love with Morgana, she was ready to do anything to save you from her corrupting influence."

Alex looked astounded. "I wish I could believe that," he murmured.

"Oh, it was true before," his father noted. "The question is whether it is still true. Or have you successfully botched your chance at happiness?"

They sat in silence while the clock loudly ticked

the minutes away. His Grace suddenly stood up. "Alex," he said hesitantly. His son looked up. "I know that we have had our differences, and advice from me is probably the last thing you want, but I have to say it anyway. Don't let pride or anger stand in your way. Do whatever you have to do to win Elizabeth back. The knowledge that you have had the last word is very poor company on cold winter evenings," he said bitterly.

Alex looked at him in surprise, but his father did not meet his eyes. Instead he picked up his glass and finished the last of his brandy. The clock was chiming midnight. "I will go up and see how Elizabeth is," he said as he put down his glass. "Margaret has had enough time to calm her down."

After his father left the room, Alex wandered over to the liquor cabinet and poured himself another brandy. How was he going to convince Elizabeth that it did not matter why he had married her, since he loved her now? Would she even bother to listen to him?

He picked up his glass and held it to his lips, but a noise from below made him stop. It almost sounded as if a carriage had stopped in front of the house. But that was ridiculous. Everyone was home, and midnight was hardly the time for anyone to be leaving. Or was it?

He slammed the glass down onto the cabinet and raced across the room. He flung open the door and ran down the stairs two at a time. He reached the sidewalk in front of the house just in time to grab the bag away from Elizabeth as she was handing it to the carriage driver. Alex tossed it to a stunned footman.

"What the hell are you doing?" he shouted at Elizabeth while Margaret cowered nearby.

"Leaving," she said coldly. She started to turn back to the coach, but he grabbed her arm and pulled her back.

"Just like that?" he cried. "Without a word?"

"I didn't think we had anything to say," she snapped.

"You may have nothing to say, but I have a great deal to say!" he informed her angrily. "And you are going to listen to it!"

She shrugged her shoulders carelessly. "Say what you like," she allowed. "I can leave a little later."

Alex's lips tightened angrily, but he said nothing, just increased his hold on her arm and pulled her toward the house.

Rather than make a scene, Elizabeth went along with him. Margaret followed, a worried look on her face.

"You can dismiss the carriage," Alex told his butler as they went into the house.

"Come back in an hour," Elizabeth called over Alex's shoulder to the coachman, ignoring both Alex and the butler.

Biting off an angry retort, Alex pushed Elizabeth up the stairs and into the library, holding the door open for Margaret to enter also. "I probably should go to my own room," she said uncertainly.

"Nonsense," Alex said as he closed the door behind her. "Someone had better stay with us. We may come to blows if we are left alone."

That did not greatly reassure Margaret, but she hurried to a nearby chair, glancing sympathetically at her daughter.

Elizabeth was standing defiantly in the middle of the room. "Well, let's hear all these wonderful things that you have to say," she snapped.

Alex held onto his temper, although it was not easy. "First of all, I want it understood that I will not have my wife running off. I would lock you in your room first."

"How loving of you!" she said sarcastically.

Alex bit his lip. Drat! That had been a stupid thing to say. He was not going to convince her that he loved her by shouting. Taking a deep breath, he continued more quietly. "Actually I would hope that you would not want to leave."

She said nothing, just continued to glare at him.

"Won't you at least sit down?" he cried in exasperation. When she looked about her for a chair, he led her over to one that was soft and comfortable. Perhaps it would help her relax and listen more amiably to him.

"I admit that I was not very honest with you before we were married," he said hesitantly, watching her closely for any change of expression. There was none, so he went on. "But you must realize yourself how my feelings have changed since then."

"Oh?" she asked skeptically.

"Look at all the clothes I helped select for you," he pointed out. "Most husbands would not go to that much trouble."

"They would if they were ashamed of their wives' appearances," she pointed out.

He ran his fingers through his hair. "I bought you the pearls."

"And the bracelet for Morgana."

"Damn it anyway! You are determined not to believe me!" he accused her bitterly, striding angrily about the room, his arms waving about him for emphasis. "On the basis of a few words from a woman who hates you, you are ready to leave me!"

"Oh, this is pointless!" Elizabeth said in disgust as she stood up. "I would like nothing better than to believe that you care about me, but I have to be realistic and face the facts. You married me as a joke."

"But I'm not laughing!" he cried. He took hold of her upper arms and looked down at her, as if by the sheer force of his will, he could make her believe him.

She twisted free from his grasp and moved a few steps away from him. "Why should I believe anything you say now?" she sneered. "You forget that I saw your great charm in action in Welford, when you could convince anybody of anything with your lies."

"That's your proof, then!" he cried, swinging his arms open wide. She stared at him blankly, and he took a step closer.

"Don't you see." His voice was soft and husky. "I could make you believe anything before because I had any lie I could think of at my disposal. Now all I've got is the truth, and look at me—all that great charm is gone. I'm shouting constantly, arguing in front of the servants. I can't convince anybody of anything because I won't resort to lies."

"That proves nothing," Elizabeth argued, but some of the anger and coldness was gone from her voice.

Alex took another step closer and took one of her hands. "If I am still lying, I ought to be able to manipulate you now as I did in Welford. I should be able to make you believe whatever I want. Instead, I just have to stand here and wait for you to decide my fate."

He looked at her face, but her eyes were cast downward. Very gently he put his hand under her chin and raised her head. Her eyes were swimming with tears, but the cold, forbidding look in them was gone.

"Oh, Libby," he whispered. "After this past week, how could you doubt that I love you?"

"You never told me," she said weakly.

Alex pulled her into his arms, forgetting totally that her mother was still in the room. "Then I had better tell you now," he said with a soft laugh. "I love you. I love you. I love you," he said, smiling down into her face. Then he bent his head and gently kissed her lips.

Margaret coughed quietly to remind them of her presence. Just as they reluctantly pulled apart, the door opened and His Grace walked in. He was carrying the Herriad Necklace in one hand and a piece of paper in the other.

"What is that?" Alex asked.

His father glanced over at him. "The Herriad Necklace," he said almost absently. His eyes were fixed on Margaret.

She bit her lip nervously and looked as if she was about to faint. She glanced around her, feeling horribly vulnerable so far away from Alex and Elizabeth.

"I'm afraid that I don't really understand," His Grace said slowly. He glanced down at the note, then up again at Margaret. "Why would you think I would want it back?" he asked her.

"Well, it's yours," Margaret tried to explain. "I didn't mean to have it."

"You didn't mean to have it?" he repeated dumbly.

Margaret flashed a worried glance at Elizabeth, who hurried over to her mother's side. "It was only by accident that she kept it," Elizabeth explained to him. Her mother stood up, clinging tightly to her hand. "Actually Mother wanted to return it, but Father stopped her."

His Grace stared at the two of them with a frown.

He rubbed the back of his head wearily as he walked over to a chair close to them and sat down.

"I don't understand where the necklace came from," Alex complained, but no one bothered to explain anything to him.

"You seem to know a great deal about this," His Grace said quietly to Elizabeth.

"Mother told me what happened," she admitted warily.

His Grace nodded slowly. "And just what did she tell you?"

Elizabeth glanced reassuringly at her mother, then back at His Grace. "She told me that she forgot she was wearing it, and when she discovered it, Father told her it was too late to send it back. That you would never forgive her and would probably have her arrested."

"Arrested?" Alex cried. "For what?"

Elizabeth turned toward him. "For stealing the necklace," she said simply.

His Grace looked hard at Margaret. "And did you really believe that I would do that?" he asked in astonishment.

"You were very angry," she reminded him timidly.

"But to have you arrested!" He could not believe that she would think such a thing of him.

"It wasn't so hard to believe," Elizabeth argued. "Look at the time you came to see us after Father died. You did not seem very concerned about us."

246

"What did you think—that I had come for the necklace?" he cried.

Margaret nodded.

"What else could we think?" Elizabeth defended them. "Our clothing was the cheapest possible, and the house was shabby beyond belief. We couldn't even offer you a decent tea! But you did not seem to care at all."

His Grace was pale as he shook his head in stunned disbelief. "I never noticed." He looked at Margaret. "I only remember how upset you seemed at Timothy's death, and it seemed wrong for me to be there."

"Of course I was upset," Margaret said quietly. "We were all alone and had no income that I knew of, and then when you came . . ." She closed her eyes briefly. "Well, I thought since Timothy was no longer there to protect me, you were going to make trouble over the necklace."

His Grace stood up and turned away. "My God! You all certainly have a fine opinion of me." He turned around. "Why didn't you suspect Alex of coming after the fool thing, too? Who knows, maybe I had sent him for it!"

Margaret and Elizabeth exchanged uneasy glances.

"I think they did," Alex remarked, but he did not seem angry. "Why didn't you just give it back to me, though?" he asked. "Surely you must have realized that once we had the necklace back, we would not have done anything to you."

"It wasn't quite that simple," Elizabeth said uneasily, finding it difficult to meet his eyes. "You see, over the past few years, since Father died, I had . . ." She gulped suddenly. "I sold some of the diamonds. When you came to Welford there were six paste stones in the necklace."

"You sold some of the diamonds!" His Grace cried, jumping to his feet.

"It was my fault," Margaret insisted. "If I had been a better mother . . ."

"But why didn't you come to me," His Grace continued. "If you had just told me, I would have been happy to help you!"

Margaret stared at him in surprise, but Elizabeth was not so dumbfounded. "Ask you for help?" she cried. "When you barely spoke civilly to us?"

"Which of the stones are paste?" Alex interrupted them. Elizabeth turned toward him. He was holding the necklace up to the light and looking at each of the stones. "They must be excellent copies," he laughed.

Glancing up suddenly, he saw Elizabeth's strained look. "Of course," he cried quietly. "Six stones! That's where Morgana's paste stones came from!"

Elizabeth nodded, a worried look on her face, but Alex shook his head with a smile. "I do believe that Morgana met her match in you!"

"What are you talking about?" his father asked in confusion.

Alex just shook his head. He picked up the necklace and turned it over in his hand. "But what I don't understand," he said as he put the necklace back down, "is how Margaret got it in the first place."

"I gave it to her," His Grace said, looking directly at Margaret. She blushed and looked down at the floor.

"You gave it to her?" Alex cried, completely puzzled. He looked at the necklace again. "But I thought . . . isn't this the one . . ."

"Quite so," his father agreed, his eyes never leaving Margaret's face. "It's the betrothal necklace."

"Betrothal!" Elizabeth shrieked. She dropped her hand and took a step back. "Mother! Is that true?"

Margaret nodded, her face still downward and her hands clenched tightly before her. "Yes," she whispered.

"And minutes after she agreed to marry me, she was out in the garden with my cousin!" His Grace informed them angrily. "No doubt planning their elopement!"

Margaret shook her head and raised her eyes to look across at him. "No, it wasn't that at all," she whispered. "You had refused to increase Timothy's allowance, and he was very angry. I was afraid that he was going to make a scene and spoil our evening, so I tried to reason with him."

His Grace looked highly skeptical. "And why didn't you tell me all that that night?" he asked.

"I tried," Margaret said. "But you wouldn't listen."

Alex laughed harshly. "Surely you don't mean my quiet and understanding father would not listen?"

His Grace glared at them all. "That doesn't explain why you eloped," he pointed out.

"You said such terrible things to me. I was certain that you'd never forgive me."

"Confound it!" His Grace cried. "You make me sound like a monster! I was never so unforgiving as you all seem to think."

"No," Margaret sighed. "But I was only seventeen, and incredibly stupid."

During the long silence that followed, Alex looked from his father to Margaret. Suddenly he took Elizabeth's arm. "If you both will excuse us, I think we've had enough excitement for one day," he said as he pulled her toward the door.

Margaret's eyes beseeched Elizabeth to stay, but Elizabeth was watching Alex. "I have to lock my wife in her room," he said with a laugh as he pushed her out the door. "Good night," he called to his father and Margaret. Then he closed the door.

The silence in the room was almost a tangible presence. Margaret wished that she had the courage to say good night also and leave, but instead she sat down on the edge of her chair and stared at the floor. When His Grace moved, she started and glanced up quickly. He was not coming closer to her, though, but had walked over to the table where the necklace lay. He picked it up.

"This really is yours, you know," he said quietly. "I would like it if you would take it back." He had not looked at her but was staring at the necklace in his hand.

Margaret stood up. "No, I don't think so," she said quietly. His Grace turned to look at her. His eyes seemed disappointed. "I think it ought to go to Elizabeth. Besides, it holds too many unhappy memories for me."

His Grace's hand closed around the necklace. "Yes, I can understand your feelings," he said quietly. "It was stupid of me to ask."

His remark seemed so final that she turned toward the door.

"After hating me for twenty years, it was foolish to think you might still care," he went on.

Margaret stopped where she was and turned around slowly to face him. "What are you saying?" she whispered.

His Grace glared at her. "I was just saying that I understand why you don't want to marry me," he snapped impatiently.

"But you didn't ask me to marry you!" she pointed out.

"I offered you the family betrothal necklace. What did you think I meant?" he cried. Suddenly his impatience vanished. "Did you mean that when you refused the necklace, you were just refusing the necklace, not me, too?" he asked, his voice full of hope.

"I just don't want the necklace," she whispered.

He moved slowly forward until he was right before her. "But what about me?" he asked. "I know I yell too much, have far too much pride and an unyielding nature, but I do still love you. Even more than I did before, if that's possible. Will you take the chance and marry me?"

He opened his arms, and Margaret moved into them as if she belonged there. He slowly folded his arms around her, hugging her close, and lightly kissed the top of her head.

"I don't know why you want to bother with someone as foolish as I am," she sighed. "I always seem to misunderstand everything."

"Just so long as you understand how much I love you," he whispered as he bent down to meet her lips.

The Herriad Necklace slipped unnoticed from his hand and fell to the soft carpet. The stones gleamed brightly in the soft firelight, but it lay where it had landed, forgotten by everyone.

When You Want A Little More Than Romance—

Try A Candlelight Ecstasy!

Dell **Wherever paperback books are sold!**

The unforgettable saga of a magnificent family

IN JOY AND IN SORROW

by

JOAN JOSEPH

They were the wealthiest Jewish family in Portugal, masters of Europe's largest shipping empire. Forced to flee the scourge of the Inquisition that reduced their proud heritage to ashes, they crossed the ocean in a perilous voyage. Led by a courageous, beautiful woman, they would defy fate to seize a forbidden dream of love.

A Dell Book   **$3.50**   **(14367-5)**

At your local bookstore or use this handy coupon for ordering:

| **Dell** | DELL BOOKS   IN JOY AND IN SORROW $3.50   (14367-5)
P.O. BOX 1000, PINE BROOK, N.J. 07058-1000 |

Please send me the books I have checked above. I am enclosing $_____ (please add 75c per copy to cover postage and handling). Send check or money order—no cash or C.O.D.'s. Please allow up to 8 weeks for shipment.

Mr./Mrs./Miss_____

Address_____

City_____State/Zip_____

The second volume in the spectacular Heiress series

The Cornish Heiress

by Roberta Gellis
bestselling author of
The English Heiress

Meg Devoran—by night the flame-haired smuggler, Red Meg. Hunted and lusted after by many, she was loved by one man alone...

Philip St. Eyre—his hunger for adventure led him on a desperate mission into the heart of Napoleon's France.

From midnight trysts in secret smugglers' caves to wild abandon in enemy lands, they pursued their entwined destinies to the end—seizing ecstasy, unforgettable adventure—and love.

A Dell Book   **$3.50**   **(11515-9)**

At your local bookstore or use this handy coupon for ordering:

Dell | **DELL BOOKS**   **THE CORNISH HEIRESS**   **$3.50**   **(11515-9)**
P.O. BOX 1000, PINE BROOK, N.J. 07058-1000

Please send me the books I have checked above. I am enclosing $ _____ (please add 75c per copy to cover postage and handling). Send check or money order—no cash or C.O.D.'s. Please allow up to 8 weeks for shipment.

Mr./Mrs./Miss _____

Address _____

City _____ State/Zip _____

Danielle Steel

AMERICA'S LEADING LADY OF ROMANCE REIGNS OVER ANOTHER BESTSELLER

A Perfect Stranger

A flawless mix of glamour and love by Danielle Steel, the bestselling author of *The Ring*, *Palomino* and *Loving*.

A DELL BOOK $3.50   #17221-7

At your local bookstore or use this handy coupon for ordering:

Dell **DELL BOOKS**   A PERFECT STRANGER $3.50   #17221-7
P.O. BOX 1000, PINE BROOK, N.J. 07058-1000

Please send me the above title. I am enclosing $_____ (please add 75¢ per copy to cover postage and handling). Send check or money order—no cash or C.O.D.'s. Please allow up to 8 weeks for shipment.

Mr. Mrs. Miss _____

Address _____

City _____ State/Zip _____